GABRIEL'S
TRIUMPH

GABRIEL'S TRIUMPH

ALISON HART

Ω
Published by
PEACHTREE PUBLISHERS
1700 Chattahoochee Avenue
Atlanta, Georgia 30318-2112
www.peachtree-online.com

Cover design by Loraine M. Joyner
Book design by Melanie McMahon Ives

Photo credits: p. 155, courtesy of the Library of Congress; p.156, courtesy of the National
Archives; p. 160, courtesy of the Historian's Office at Hilton, NY.

Printed in the United States of America
10 9 8 7 6 5 4 3 2 1
First Edition

Library of Congress Cataloging-in-Publication Data
Library of Congress Cataloging-in-Publication Data

Hart, Alison, 1950-
  Gabriel's triumph / by Alison Hart. -- 1st ed.
    p. cm.
  Summary: A thirteen-year-old newly freed slave faces the challenges of freedom and
horse racing as he pursues his dream of becoming a famous jockey in Civil War Kentucky
and New York.
  ISBN 978-1-56145-410-5
  [1. Jockeys--Fiction. 2. Horse racing--Fiction. 3. Freedmen--Fiction. 4. African Americans-
-Fiction. 5. United States--History--Civil War, 1861-1865--Fiction.] I. Title.
  PZ7.H256272Gd 2007
  [Fic]--dc22
                                                2007001430

To hard-riding jockeys and their fast-racing mounts,
from past to present.

—A. H.

LIST OF CHARACTERS

KENTUCKY

Gabriel Alexander—a 13-year-old former slave, now a groom
and jockey at Woodville Farm

Lucy Alexander—Gabriel's mother, a former house slave at
Woodville Farm

Isaac Alexander—Gabriel's father, a trainer at Woodville Farm
who enlisted in the Union army and is now stationed at
Camp Nelson.

Jase and Tandy—grooms at Woodville Farm

Annabelle—a 13-year-old house slave at Woodland Farm and a
friend of Gabriel's

Mister Winston Giles—owner of Woodville Farm

Mistress Jane Giles—mistress of Woodville Farm

Renny—a coachman at Woodville Farm

Old Uncle—a slave who cares for the yard and garden
at Woodville Farm

Major Wiley—owner of a neighboring farm

One Arm Dan Parmer—a Rebel (Confederate) guerilla and
head of an outlaw band

Butler and Keats—Rebel guerillas

Newcastle—a trainer from the North who once worked at
Woodville Farm

Captain Waite—captain of the Company D cavalry from Camp
Nelson

Saratoga Springs, New York

Mister Baker—stable manager at the Saratoga Race Course

Short Bit—a young worker for Mister Baker

Cornelius Jeremiah—a racehorse owner

Hooks and Cuffy—grooms for Mister Jeremiah

Gordon and Danny—workers at the stables

Jackson—Gabriel's friend and a former jockey at Woodville Farm, now riding for Doctor Crown

Abe Hawkins—a famous African American jockey

Gilpatrick—a famous Irish jockey

CHAPTER ONE

July 1864

Huff...*huff*...*huff*... The colt gallops toward the grandstand, puffing like a steam engine arriving at the Lexington depot. It's the final mile of the second heat, and Captain Conrad's running so fine, I can't quit grinning.

I peer over my left shoulder. Jane's Delight is a nose behind, but the mare's tight against the rail and coming on. Chirping, I urge Captain ahead. Don't want Jane's jockey hooking my stirrup and flipping me off. A rider who falls in the middle of a race might likely be trampled bloody.

Shouts pummel us as the horses race past the grandstand:

"Ram the spurs into Lord Fairfax! Rowel him up!"

"Come on, Grey Eagle!"

"Pull Jane steady!"

"Use the whip, boy!"

I don't hear Mister Giles hollering. Before the race he told me to ride Captain smart, and that's what I'm doing.

Crouched low, I canter Captain around the turn and down the backstretch of the Kentucky Association track. As we head into the dip, I note the rest of the horses falling behind. My fingers are bloody from holding the reins so tight, my throat's dry, and my legs tremble from the strain of galloping three and a half miles. But pride's swelling in my chest. Ain't no horse going to eat up that distance. Ain't no horse about to beat me and Captain now!

Mister Giles says he'll pay me fifty dollars if I win.

Fifty dollars!

That's a dream come true to a colored boy like me.

My mind's on the purse money when I see a blur of motion to my right. Lord Fairfax is charging from out of nowhere!

Foolish thoughts of money may cost me the race.

Adam, Lord Fairfax's jockey, flails the whip brutally against his horse's flank. Adam's got a wild spark in his eye, and I figure that whip will soon find me. I hunch lower to drive Captain on. Then I feel a rough bump, and Captain lurches left. Grabbing mane, I barely keep from pitching off.

I glance to my right. Lord Fairfax is neck and neck with Captain. Our stirrup irons touch, and Adam yanks his left rein, forcing Lord Fairfax to bump Captain again.

We hit hard, throwing Captain off his stride.

I frown. Adam *ain't* going to bump me again.

I ain't going to lose fifty dollars because of no cheating jockey, neither.

Gritting my teeth, I perch my hands high on Captain's

mane. "Run on, fine colt," I croon hoarsely. "Run on like we're chasing those Rebels."

I purse my lips and squeeze my boot heels into his sides. Captain springs forward, righting his gait. His front legs stretch high and long, grabbing the track as he thunders around the homestretch bend, pelting that no-account Adam with clumps of dirt. Roars erupt from the grandstand as we fly past the finish-line pole.

I raise my fist in the air. It's my second race—and my second win!

How I wish Pa and my friend Jackson could see me. But both are far away. Jackson's racing Thoroughbreds in a place called Saratoga. Pa's in the Union army at Camp Nelson.

Captain slows to a trot, and I'm deafened with cheers. The men who placed bets must be pleased with the results of the race. When I turn Captain, I spot Mister Giles hurrying down the grandstand steps. One hand secures his top hat against the wind, the other holds his cane.

Then a *yahoo* rends the air, and Jase shoots from between the men hanging over the track's railing. He lands in the dirt, beats his bare black feet on the ground like a victory drum, and runs to my side.

"You did it, Gabriel!" he cries as he loops a rope through Captain's snaffle ring.

"We did it." I lay my palm against Captain's slick neck. The colt's nostrils are flared, but his breathing's clear, so I know he ain't too winded to enjoy his victory. "Captain and me. And you helped, too, Jase."

Jase is little and skinny. He's Captain's groom, but when

he's thirteen—as old as me—he's going to be a jockey, too.

"I did help, didn't I?" Jase throws back his bony shoulders and struts over to the judges' stand, leading Captain. "Ain't *no* horse can beat *my* colt."

I chuckle. I don't want to stomp on Jase's bragging, but I know one horse that can beat Captain: *Aristo.* That colt's so fast he can outrun the wind. And soon I aim to race him—and win, too.

Mister Giles strides to the judges' stand. "Well done, Gabriel Alexander!" He reaches up to shake my hand.

Like I'm a man, I think.

I shake back, my fingers leaving bloody smudges on his doeskin gloves. Mister Giles joins the track president and the mayor of Lexington, who present him with an engraved plate and the purse money. All around us, there's so much cheering that it's hard to believe there's a war raging between the North and the South.

Licking my swollen lips, I crack a smile for the crowd. A reporter from the *Lexington Observer* asks Mister Giles questions about Captain Conrad. Beside him, a second man draws on a pad. "Hey, boy!" he calls up to me. "Jump off that horse. I need a sketch of him for the paper."

My smile fades. After a race, there's plenty of glory for the winning horse. And glory for the owner. But no glory for the jockey.

Jackson warned me after my first race. "Gabriel," he said, a stalk of straw waggling between his teeth, "Kentucky's a slave state. Reporters don't write my name in the paper, and I been racing for two years. They write 'Mister Giles's colored jockey' or 'the darky rider.' I don't let it get to me, and you shouldn't, either."

That's one reason why Jackson left Kentucky for Saratoga, New York. He's hoping to find fame in the North.

One day, I vow, *I'll find fame, too.*

Jase leads us outside the track railing. I slip off Captain's back. My legs buckle, and when the colt rubs his sweaty head on my shoulder, he tumbles me clean off my feet.

I land hard on the ground and my racing cap falls into my lap. Jase twitches with laughter, but I'm too tuckered to yell at him. If Pa were here, he'd have caught me before I fell.

Jase loosens Captain's girth and walks him toward the barn. After slapping the dirt off my breeches with my cap, I hobble after them. Pa's old boots have rubbed my feet raw. Captain's got a hitch in his front leg, and I wonder if that last bump hurt him.

When we reach the barn, Renny, Mister Giles's coachman, hurries over. "Won me some coins betting on you and Captain," he says gleefully. "They're burnin' a hole in my pocket, so I'm headin' into town." He lowers his head and his voice. "Don't be tellin' Master where I gone, Gabriel. If he asks, tell him I'm gettin' the wagon wheel looked at."

He slips off into the milling crowd, and I shake my head in disgust. "Ain't going to lie for you, Renny," I say to his departing shadow. Ever since Pa left to join the army, Renny's taken to playing poker all night and staggering back to the barn with empty pockets.

Bending over, I run my hand down Captain's pasterns.

There's heat and a slight swelling above the right front fetlock.

"Horse needs time in the stream," I tell Jase as I sink down on a wooden box and pull off Pa's boots. There are blisters on my toes and heels. Maybe I'll use this win money to buy me some boots.

Wearily, I lean against the barn wall. But it's a short rest, 'cause I hear Pa's voice in my head: *Colt just ran four hard miles for you, Gabriel. Least you can do is see to his care.*

Pa has magic ways with horses. Folks say I've got the magic, too. Only I tell them it ain't magic. Horses tell you what they need. Pa and me, why, we just listen.

"Captain could beat any horse in Kentucky!" Jase's boasting cuts into my thoughts.

I look up. Several gentlemen in frock coats are strolling by, admiring Captain's glossy brown coat and white star. One of them comes over to where I'm resting, and I jump to my feet.

"Fine riding," he tells me. He's got a black goatee and a fat paunch that strains his vest buttons. I remember him from the first time I raced at the track. *That's Doctor Rammer,* Pa had said. *A man who whips his horses as hard as his slaves.*

Hooking his thumbs in his pockets, Doctor Rammer leans back and studies me. "A boy like you could make some money riding *my* Thoroughbreds."

"No thank you, sir."

"Why not, may I ask? You're free now, I believe." He

wags one finger at me. "And your pa's left Woodville Farm for the army."

"Yes sir. But I'm riding Mister Winston Giles's Thoroughbreds." I don't tell him the real reason I said no. I'd never work for a man who wields a whip.

Doctor Rammer harrumphs. "My Thoroughbreds are the finest in Kentucky. And I just hired a new trainer from the North. So when you get tired of riding Winston's broken-down nags, Gabriel, come see me."

"When crows turn white," I mutter when he walks off. But secretly, I'm feeling proud. Three weeks ago, I was a slave with no name. Two wins later, I'm a jockey named Gabriel and men are asking me to race their Thoroughbreds. How many more wins before I'm famous?

A crowd of ladies strolls past, parasols twirling over their shoulders. Jase is staring at them, but my gaze is drawn to the man walking behind the ladies. He's wearing a slouch hat, a dusty gray jacket, and spurs on the heels of his grimy boots.

A Rebel guerrilla!

Instinctively, I touch my upper arm. Under my jockey silks, I feel the crusted scar from that Rebel bullet. I tense, my eyes frozen on the man, fear scattering thoughts of glory from my head.

CHAPTER TWO

Is the man a raider from One Arm Dan Parmer's band? *No, he can't be,* I quickly tell myself, my eyes still tight on him. The Union army clapped those no-goods in the Federal jail.

Then I realize the man's wearing tan buckskin, not Confederate gray. Even if he was a raider, though, he wouldn't dare wear a Rebel uniform in Lexington. Early in the war, the town waved the Confederate flag. But now Union soldiers are camped everywhere, and Rebels have to skulk in the shadows.

Still, my mind's buzzing with suspicion. The man's got a revolver stuck in his belt, and he's eyeing Captain hungrily. I ain't taking a chance. Rebel guerrillas are drawn to Thoroughbreds like flies to manure.

I jump forward. "Quit bragging and get the colt's halter," I snap at Jase, who's showing off Captain to the admiring ladies. Keeping my eyes on the stranger, I snatch Captain's rope from Jase and snug the colt's head to my side.

The man halts, places his hand on the butt of his gun, and

gives me a toothless sneer. "What're you so afraid of, boy?"

I drop my chin. My fingers tighten around the rope, and I dare not look up at him. A black boy ain't nothing but a target for a white Rebel's hate.

He leans close, and I smell whiskey on his breath. "Cat got yer tongue?" he asks.

"Move along, sir," someone says, and I recognize Mister Giles's voice.

"Ain't harmin' no one," the man mutters, but he stalks off, spurs jingling, and relief washes over me like cold river water.

Mister Giles places his hand on my shoulder. "Fine race, Gabriel. Jackson and your pa would be proud. I believe you earned this." Several bills are cradled in his palm. "Fifty dollars. Spend it wisely."

I lick my parched lips. "Thank you, sir."

My fingers tremble as I reach for the money. The first money I've earned as a free man. After I helped save Woodville Farms' Thoroughbreds from One Arm and his raiders, Mister Giles gave me my freedom.

Up to now, free life ain't been much different from slave life. I'm still riding and tending racehorses at Woodville Farm, and even though I ain't got a master now, I have to mind Mister Giles, Ma and Pa. But *fifty dollars,* that can change any man. I've seen what powerful things money can do to a sensible fellow. Look at Jackson and Renny. One took off for the North and the other follows every poker game he hears about. What might it do to me, a boy who's tasting his first bite of freedom and riches?

I drop my empty hand to my side. "Please, sir. Give it to my ma. She'll keep it safe."

"Wise decision." He pockets the bills. "How's Captain?"

"Mister Giles? Mister Winston Giles?" A white boy runs over, waving a sheet of paper. Suspenders hold up his knee-length britches. A straw hat is perched on his head.

"I'm Winston Giles."

"Telegraph for you, sir."

Mister Giles tosses the boy a coin and takes the telegraph. As he reads, his face pales under the brim of his top hat. "My wife has taken a turn for the worse," he tells me. "We need to ride back tonight. If we ride hard, we should make it home by sundown."

"Sir, Captain can't take a hard ride. The colt's got swelling in his right front leg. Lord Fairfax bumped us mighty hard."

"I can't delay. You, Jase, and Renny will have to stay the night and rest Captain. Load up the wagon in the morning and bring the colt home then. I'll rent a carriage and driver in town."

"Yes sir." My chest tightens at the thought of the ride back to Woodville Farm. When the Yankee cavalry went after the Rebel raiders, their leader, One Arm, got away. What if we run into him on our ride home? The Rebel bullet that tore up my arm came from One Arm's rifle. I faced him once and almost got myself killed. I ain't excited about doing it again.

"One Arm is in Missouri by now, Gabriel," Mister Giles says, as if he reads the worry in my face. "I trust you with

Captain's care. I have no choice but to head home immediately. Mistress Jane is gravely ill." Touching his hat brim,
he hastens off.

As soon as he leaves, I scold myself for my cowardly
thoughts. I should be thinking on Ma and Annabelle. Ma's
been caring for Mistress Jane for months, and Annabelle's
like a daughter to the mistress. Both of them will take it
hard if she dies.

I unbuckle Captain's girth. Jase trots up, the halter slung
over one shoulder. "I'll take Captain."

"No, I need to wash him and soak his legs in the
stream." I slide the saddle off the colt's sweaty back. "You go
clean his stall and put in fresh hay. Then wipe his saddle and
bridle."

Jase folds his arms against his ribs, all stubborn like. "You
ain't my master, Gabriel. I ain't gonna follow your orders."

"Yes, you will. I'm your boss until Renny comes back
from town. Mistress Jane's taken a turn for the worse and
Mister Giles has gone to Woodville."

Jase's eyes grow round as buttons. "Gone?"

"You, me, and Renny will bring Captain home tomorrow."

"But what about the raiders?"

"The raiders are all gone or in jail, Jase," I say firmly.
"And Renny'll be with us."

"Renny ain't got a gun. He's just a slave like me."

"Well, he's also a man. We'll make it safely home tomorrow, I promise." I hand the saddle to Jase, then pat the boy's
skinny shoulder. Jase was at Woodville the day the raiders
came, and even though he didn't get shot, his fear is as real

11

as mine. That's why I repeat with as much bravado as I can muster, "We'll make it home just fine."

★★★

The creak of wagon wheels wakes me. Yawning, I rub the straw dust from my eyes and kick off the blanket. It's already getting hot, and the day ain't hardly begun yet. Sitting up on my pallet, I listen to the sounds of the racetrack.

Outside the barn, horses snort and a rooster crows. The top door of the stall is open. The sky is dove gray, so I know it ain't sunrise yet. I think about lying back down, but I shake off the thought and struggle to my feet. We have a long journey ahead of us today.

I tuck my shirt into my homespun britches and brush the straw from my hair. My feet are scabby and my legs ache, and I wince with each step. Peering over the stall door, I glance right and left.

Something seems wrong, but for a moment the reason escapes me.

Then it hits me: *The wagon's gone!*

Whipping around, I stare at the corner of the stall where Renny laid his pallet last night.

Pallet's gone. Pack's gone. Renny's gone, too.

He's hitching up the horses, I tell myself as I swing open the stall door. But I know he's not there. Last night when Renny came back from town and heard that Mister Giles had left for home, he was mighty quiet for a while. Then he told me and Jase to get a good night's sleep so we could get an early start in the morning. *He was already plotting his escape,* I think. *I should have known it from that faraway gleam in his eye.*

I hurry to the pole corral at the end of the barn. Mister Giles's team of wagon horses is gone, too.

It's eight miles from Lexington to Woodville Farm. Jase and me will have to travel it on our own.

Panic grips my empty stomach. But I don't blame Renny for running away. This war has given slaves a chance for freedom. I saw it at Camp Nelson when Jackson took me to visit Pa. Slaves from all over Kentucky had streamed into camp to enlist in the Union army, gladly exchanging an overseer and a hoe for a sergeant and a rifle.

Might be Renny's gone to join Pa. If I weren't free already, would I steal off, too?

I tried to enlist at Camp Nelson, but Pa told me I was too young. If you ask me, young *and* old should be fighting for freedom. And that's what I aim to do as soon as... *Well, as soon as Ma lets me,* I think sheepishly. Ma doesn't want both her men fighting and dying in the war. Besides, there's also that important matter of me becoming a famous jockey.

"Jesus, watch over Renny and help him find freedom," I pray before turning back to Captain's stall. The colt has stuck his head over the half door. He whickers hungrily. "My gut's rumbling, too," I tell him as I scratch the white star under his forelock. Jase is curled beneath a blanket in the far corner of the stall, snoring softly.

I toss Captain an armful of hay, then shake the last of the grain from the sack into his feed bucket. When I set the bucket over the door, Jase wakes up. He stands groggily and leans against Captain's side, his blanket wrapped around his bony shoulders. Straw pokes from his hair, and his eyes are wide with worry.

"Renny's gone, ain't he?" he says.

"He's gone and there ain't nothing we can do 'bout it." I open the stall door. "So come on, we got to get ready to start home."

"Alone?"

"Not alone. You have me and I have you." I stride down the shed row to the supply stall.

"That's s'posed to make me feel better?" he calls. I hear Captain's stall door slam shut and Jase's footsteps hurrying after me. I'm as scared as he is, but I'm trying to hide it. Trying to think and act like Pa.

Feed Captain, groom him, check his legs, tack him up, pack up supplies. I list the chores in my head, but when I halt outside the supply stall and look inside, I realize the foolishness of my last words. Renny's run off with the horses, the wagon, and the supplies.

Tears threaten. I blink them back. *You ain't a child no more, Gabriel, so don't be crying.* "Looks like Renny took *everything,* Jase."

"He didn't take everything." Darting into the stall, Jase stoops near the back corner. "Renny left us a basket of food!" He lifts it up by the handle and excitedly points out the contents like we're going on a picnic, not a dangerous journey. "Lookee, there's a hunk of Cook Nancy's bread, two hoecakes, a tin for water, and a chunk of cheese." He grins. "Lucky Renny left it for us. Bet he knew we'd be hungry."

I keep my lips tight, letting Jase believe that Renny left the basket. The truth is, before bedding down last night I packed the food. Must be I knew in my heart that Renny would be gone by daybreak.

"We'll pack the food and the blankets. We need to travel light," I tell Jase, who's stuffing a hoecake into his mouth. "Best save the rest for later or we'll get mighty hungry on our trip." Shoulders bowed, I head back to Captain's stall. The colt's finished his grain and is plowing through his hay, hungry after yesterday's race. By now, the rest of the barn folks are stirring. There's a second meet today, but we'll be long gone. Before One Arm and his guerrillas came to Woodville, Mister Giles was planning on bringing a half dozen Thoroughbreds for this two-day meet. The raid on the farm changed his plans.

I run my hand down Captain's front legs. They're tight and cool. No sign of yesterday's swelling. Least that's in our favor. The horse—and our own feet—will have to get us home.

Silently I groom Captain while he eats, letting the rhythmic strokes of the brush soothe both of us. Outside the stall, I hear Jase haggling with someone over food. When the voices grow quiet, I figure the boy's begged enough for a morning meal.

Minutes later, he peers over the stall door, crumbs sprinkling his lips. He hands me a ragged slice of bread and a wrinkled peach. My mouth waters at the sight of the sorry meal, and I thank him with a smile.

By the time we're ready to leave, the grounds of the racetrack are teeming with owners, grooms, and trainers getting their Thoroughbreds ready for the day's meet. I boost Jase onto the lightweight racing saddle. The food is bundled in one blanket and tied behind the saddle.

I wrap my boots, racing cap, and silks in the other blanket and fling the bundle over my shoulder. With eyes downcast, I lead Captain and Jase from the track grounds. As we make our way through the city of Lexington, no one pays us any mind. They don't see yesterday's winning horse or winning jockey. We're just two barefoot colored boys taking Master's horse home.

Thank the Lord they don't see our fear and worry.

★★★

The rhythmic *clip-clop-clip-clop* of Captain's hooves on the packed dirt of Frankfort Pike has lulled Jase to sleep. He's slumped in front of me in the saddle, his cheek squashed against Captain's mane. Spittle runs down his chin and he breathes easy.

I don't know how many miles we've gone, but the sun's setting and goose bumps prickle my arms. So far, our journey's been trouble free, except for a wrong turn out of town. If Annabelle had been with us, she would've read the road signs. Me, I just guessed, and we ended riding north toward Georgetown. Finding our way back added extra miles, and now I'm double sorry for the delay. I don't care to be on the pike after sundown.

I glance nervously around. The shadows are deepening along the brushy roadside. Tree boughs overhead block the late afternoon light. Captain's head is hanging, and the reins loop free. The colt's as tuckered as we are, and I feel the hitch coming back into his walk.

A twig snaps in the brush. My heart drums beneath my ribs. I gather the reins, sit higher in the saddle, and find my stirrups. Twigs have been snapping the whole journey, but when the sun was high, its warmth and brightness kept the haunts away.

Haunts. Slaves love to tell tales when the work's done and the sun's low. They rock on the porch, smoke their tobacco, and weave stories about spirits who rise from the grave to trouble the living.

Ma scolds me when I repeat the tales to her. "Stay away from those storytellers, Gabriel Alexander. Don't even listen."

But I never could resist those magical stories. Now I wish I had a charm string around my neck to ward off those spirits.

Abruptly, Captain halts and I pitch forward, knocking into Jase. The horse's ears prick as he stares down the road.

I right myself and stare in the same direction, the images of evil spirits still whirling in my head. There's a solitary horseman in the middle of the pike. In the dim light he's just a black silhouette, and I can't make out his dress or features. A chill runs down my arms, right into my fingertips.

The man's sitting there on his horse—like he's waiting for us. And he ain't no spirit.

"Jase," I whisper, giving him a shake. "Wake up. We might have to make a run for it."

He mutters sleepily, but when I pinch his shoulder he jerks upright. "Keep it down," I warn. "He might not have seen us."

Jase presses back into my chest, and I feel his body quiver. "W-who is it?" he stammers.

"Might be no one." *Might be a Rebel.*

With a soft cluck, I turn Captain around. I try to picture the countryside we just passed through. Was there a farm or house by the road that might give us refuge?

Captain breaks into a jog and his hooves sound like hammer strikes on the road. Jase jounces wildly on the pommel. I steer with one arm and hold onto his shirt with the other. I feel Captain's lameness in the lurch of his stride. If the horseman gives chase, ain't no way the colt can outrun him.

I glance over my shoulder and the sight makes me cry out.

The horseman's cantering after us!

CHAPTER THREE

Jase," I hiss in his ear. "When I rein Captain toward the side of the road, you slip off and hide in the woods."

"But Gabriel—"

"Do it!"

Digging my heel in Captain's right side, I aim the colt into the brush. Jase is still clinging to the mane, so I lift him up by his shirt. *"Hide!"* I command, before tugging him from the saddle. "Don't come out, no matter what. If anything happens, get to the farm and tell Mister Giles."

He dives from the horse into the high weeds. I hear a thud, a rustle, and then silence. I turn Captain back onto the road and urge him into a canter. The horseman's close enough that I can see the shape of his Confederate kepi cap.

I kick Captain hard.

The horse senses my fear. Lame leg and all, he stretches into a gallop. Ahead of me, another horseman drifts like a ghost into the road, blocking my escape.

Captain skids to a stop. Shaking, I blink wordlessly at this second man, who wears a slouch hat and buckskin coat. Patting the gun butt in his belt, he gives me a toothless sneer. "Howdy, boy," he says. "Fancy meeting you again."

I rein Captain around, but the Confederate in the kepi blocks my way. Behind me, I hear the cock of a gun.

"Don't try to run," barks the man in the slouch hat. "Ain't no horse can outrun a bullet."

I swallow hard. Beyond the brush, heavy woods rise on both sides of the road. Even if Captain charged into the trees, we'd soon be caught—or shot.

I'm trapped between the two riders.

The man in the slouch hat reins his horse next to Captain, his weapon resting lazily on the pommel. His horse is swaybacked; its long tail is tangled with burrs. "I believe you got something I want," the man says, as hard as winter.

I twist my fingers in Captain's mane.

"I saw your master pay you for riding." He shakes his head in disgust. "Paying *you*, a darky. Why, Yankees are *killing* us Confederates to free uppity slaves like you." He spits between Captain's front hooves. "And it's high time someone paid for my fellow Rebels' deaths." His mouth twists into a nasty grin. "Looks like that someone is you."

"I-I ain't got any money, sir," I stammer.

The man snorts. "You saying I'm a liar? Keats!" he calls to the rider in the kepi. "Find that money and prove I'm not a liar."

Keats spurs his horse beside Captain. A knife is clutched in his hand. With one swift slice, he cuts the blanket from behind the saddle and flicks it onto his pommel. He paws through it and, finding only two hoecakes, tosses it to the ground.

"Nothing in there, Butler."

"Then search the boy." Butler waves the gun at me. "Money's got to be somewhere."

"Give me that blanket on your shoulder." Keats leans closer. Caught by a ray of the setting sun, his face glows blood red.

I hesitate. The bundle holds Pa's boots and Mister Giles's racing silks. I don't want to lose either.

When I don't move fast enough, Keats snatches the blanket off my shoulder and unties it. The shirt falls to the road, and Captain skitters sideways into Butler's horse. The gun barrel swings through the air, catching me behind my ear.

Pain explodes in my head. The blow whacks me off balance, and I tumble from the saddle. I land flat on my back on the dirt road, all sense knocked out of me. Dimly, I hear voices and feel hands roughly search my clothes. Then hooves clatter off, and I drift into blackness.

★★★

"Gabriel, you all right?" Someone jostles my shoulder and my head struggles to clear. "Gabriel!" The voice sounds panicky. "Say you're alive. You got to be alive!"

I moan.

"Oh sweet Jesus, don't let him die!" the voice wails. I'm

drifting off again when something cold presses against the side of my head. The snap of cold and pain makes my eyelids fly open.

"Ye-ow!" I swat at a hand. It's pitch dark, and all I can see are the whites of Jase's eyes as he stares down at me.

"Hallelujah!" he exclaims. "You're alive! Now stop hitting me. I'm trying to cool that bump on your head." He holds up the red racing shirt, which is dripping wet. "There's a creek about ten paces off the road. I dipped your shirt in it. Thought you were never coming to."

My fingers touch behind my ear and I wince. "How long was I out?" Sitting up, I look around. It's deep night, and I can't see anything up or down the road.

"Don't worry. They're gone," Jase says.

"Where's Captain?"

"Umm." Jase's eyes shift sideways. "They took him, Gabriel. Took *everything* except the shirt and cap."

"Pa's boots?"

He nods. "I'm sorry."

"Weren't your fault." Tears well in my eyes. "Captain's lame. If they're traveling fast, he ain't going to last the night." I slap my palms on the road, sending up a cloud of dust. I'm angry at the two men, but even more infuriated with myself. "The colt raced his heart out for me, and I let the raiders take him!"

"Seems that's twice now them Rebels got the best of you, Gabriel," Jase says as he dabs at my aching head.

"Only 'cause the odds were stacked in their favor!" I say hotly.

"Don't get mad at *me*." He springs to his feet. "I'm only saying that if you don't want to keep getting bushwhacked, you need a plan. Might be you should've told them you're not some slave they can push around. That you're a winning jockey."

I snort. The boy doesn't understand. "They already know I'm a jockey, Jase. The man called Butler saw Mister Giles pay me after the race. That's why they bushwhacked us. Bet they've been following us since we left the track." My anger grows sharper. "Bet those two aren't even real Confederates. Real soldiers would be harassing Yankees, not stealing from the likes of us."

"Mister Giles paid you money?" Jase gasps. "And those Rebels stole it?"

"They didn't get my money. I asked Mister Giles to keep it for me." I swallow the sorrow rising in my throat. "But they got Captain. Ain't that bad enough?"

"Wasn't nothing you could do, Gabriel."

"If I was a Union soldier like Pa, I could have fought them."

"And I could have jumped them from the bushes. Only then we'd both be dead."

"Mister Giles trusted me with his horse!"

Jase shrugs like he knows there's nothing he can say to make it right.

I rub my aching head. I picture Captain growing as bony and raggedy as the raiders' horses. *Pa wouldn't have lost Captain.*

"I don't know how I'm going to tell Mister Giles," I say

to Jase, the thought making my head pound harder.

"You'll find a way. Now come on." Jase helps me to my feet. "We best be getting home 'fore you bleed to death."

I sway unsteadily until I get my bearings. "Shouldn't be more than a mile." I tuck the racing cap in my waistband and drape the wet shirt around my neck. "Least the raiders left Mister Giles's racing colors."

"They left one more thing." Jase pulls a crushed hoecake from his pocket and offers it to me. "I ate the other one. Couldn't help myself."

Lint and dirt are stuck to the flattened cake, but my stomach still growls hungrily at the sight. I laugh.

"What's so funny?"

"My stomach's talking to me," I reply, taking the hoecake from Jase. I set off down the road, my legs wobbly.

"Didn't know stomachs could talk. What's it sayin'?" Jase asks as he falls into step beside me.

"It's saying, 'Gabriel, I'm glad you're still alive to enjoy this hoecake'."

★★★

My feet and legs are about to give out when I spot the brick posts that mark the lane into Woodville Farm. I nudge Jase's arm. The last ten minutes, he's been quiet, like he's walking in his sleep. "Jase, we're home."

"Thank the Lord," he mumbles.

Relief quickens my pace and I jog up the lane, Jase dogtrotting behind. After One Arm and his gang raided the

farm, Mister Giles hired more armed guards and watch-
men. But no one calls out or stops us. Two foot-sore
colored boys mustn't seem much of a threat.

I slow by the picket fence that surrounds the yard of the
Main House. A candle in a lantern flickers in one of the tall
front windows, its glow casting shadows on the white
columns of the veranda. The heavy front door is closed, and
no one comes out to greet us.

No use waking Mister Giles, I decide. The bad news
about Captain can wait until morning.

"I aim to curl up in the straw and sleep forever," Jase
mutters.

"Come with me first. Ma will fix us something to eat."
Hugging the outside of the picket fence, I hurry past the
kitchen garden toward my family's cabin. It sits behind the
Main House, a hayfield away from the slave quarters.
Golden candlelight fills the lone front window, but when I
fling open the door, Ma ain't sitting in her rocker waiting
for me.

I hurry to her bedroom. The quilt's smooth on her
mattress, and the room's dark. "She must be tending Mistress
Jane," I say when I come out, only Jase doesn't respond.

I look around the room. The plank table holds a tin plate,
cup, and spoon, like Ma was waiting on me for dinner. A pail
of water sits on the counter, a washrag and chunk of soap
next to it. A pot of rabbit stew waits on the hearth.

"Jase?" I call.

I hear soft breathing. I poke my head around the sacking
that hangs from a rope, marking off my sleeping quarters in

the corner of the kitchen. Jase is sprawled face down on my ticking-covered mattress, sound asleep.

I tuck my quilt around his legs. Taking the candleholder from the table, I make my way through the kitchen garden to the back of the Main House. Ma will want to know that we made it home safely.

The coals glow in the fireplace, lighting the summer kitchen. I hurry into the Main House, tiptoeing down the long hallway. Pausing at the bottom of the winding staircase, I look up. The upstairs hall is dark and quiet.

"Gabriel, is that you?"

I whirl around, recognizing Mister Giles's voice. Holding up the candle, I peer through the arched doorway of the dark parlor. I can barely make out his hunched form sitting on the settee.

"Yes sir. It's me."

"I'm glad you made it home safely." He sounds very tired. "Come here a minute and tell me about your journey. I expected you home hours ago."

I swallow hard, knowing I have to tell him about Captain.

I set the candleholder on the hall table. Dropping my chin to my chest, I walk slowly into the parlor. My heart's hammering. I halt in front of the settee, my eyes on my dirty feet, my voice strained. "I, uh, have some bad news, sir."

"As do I." His sigh is heavy. "Mistress Jane is dying. It's only a matter of time. I couldn't bear it in her room any longer."

I clasp my hands behind me. Even though I've lived at Woodville Farm all my life, I barely know my mistress. She rarely left the house. Annabelle told me that her only interests were flowers, music, and reading.

Mister Giles clears his throat. "Now, tell me your news. Was there trouble?"

"Yes sir." I decide to start at the beginning. "When we woke this morning, Renny was gone. He'd taken the wagon, the team, and all the supplies."

The settee creaks as Mister Giles slumps back in his seat. "I was afraid that might happen. Slaves in Kentucky have been stealing off every chance they get." He looks up at me. "I'd hoped I could depend on Renny, but I suppose he saw this as a good chance to get away. And there's no use hunting for him now that sentiment is in favor of the Yankees."

"Yes sir."

"Why did it take so long for you and Jase to get here?" he asks.

"Well, sir, we took a wrong turn, and then—" My words stick in my throat. *How can I tell him his prize colt is gone?*

"Go on, Gabriel. And then?" Mister Giles prods.

"And…and then two raiders jumped us about a mile from here. Sir, I'm so sorry, but *they stole Captain!*" I press my knuckles against my mouth, trying to hold back my sobs, but they burst from my gut until my shoulders shake and my nose runs.

Mister Giles fishes a handkerchief from his pocket and hands it to me. I blow hard, embarrassed. I'm supposed to be acting like a man, not a boy.

"Don't grieve on it so, Gabriel. There are worse things than having a horse stolen."

"Yes sir," I choke out, only I ain't sure what could be worse for Captain.

"It's very late. We'll speak about this in the morning," he adds, dismissing me with a nod. "I'll let your mother know you're safe."

"Thank you, sir." I back out of the parlor into the front hall. Shrill keening comes from upstairs, and the hair rises on my arms.

It's the sound of the living mourning the dead.

Sinking to my knees on the bottom step, I bow my head and pray.

I pray that Mistress Jane finds safe passage into Heaven.

I pray for Annabelle, Ma, and Mister Giles.

And I pray for Captain.

CHAPTER FOUR

A thousand dollars reward to bring my Thoroughbred, Captain Conrad, safely home to Woodville," Mister Giles announces. He's standing under the arched trellis gateway of the picket fence. Before him, a small army of horses and riders mill about on the curved lane in front of the Main House. "Catch Butler and Keats and I'll add another five hundred."

For two days after Mistress Giles was buried, the farm was in mourning. On the third day, Mister Giles sent messengers to all the neighbors. Within a few hours, over a dozen heavily armed riders had responded. Now it's daybreak, and they're waiting to head out.

I'm in the front yard of the Main House, standing with Old Uncle under an elm tree, watching the riders. I recognize Mister Ham with his sons Henry and Beale, Major Wiley, and several of his hired hands. Major Wiley owns the farm next to Woodville Farm. A month ago, Rebel raiders stole a barn full of his horses. Only five were recovered. He doesn't want the reward money Mister Giles is offering; he wants revenge.

I want revenge, too.

"Wish I could go," I mutter to Old Uncle. Old Uncle cares for the yard and gardens around the Main House. This summer the gardens are bursting with Mistress Jane's favorite flowers. I hope she's enjoying them from Heaven.

"You want to go so you can git shot?" he asks. "Or might be you want dat reward?"

"I don't want the reward. I want to find Captain—to make up for losing him."

Old Uncle shakes his head. "Don't seem like you lost him. Seems like someone took him."

"You sound like Ma." I glance over my shoulder toward the Main House. Since Mistress Jane died, I've seen little of my ma. I spot Annabelle on the veranda, half-hidden behind a column, watching the riders, too. It's the first time I've laid eyes on her since the burial. She's wearing one of Mistress Jane's hand-me-down black dresses, and her face is dull and lifeless.

Ma tells me that Annabelle's grieving hard.

"Word has it that Butler and Keats were heading south toward Versailles," Mister Giles goes on. "The Federals believe they were part of One Arm's gang, which broke up when the majority of them were captured. Butler and Keats may be joining up with Sue Mundy's band, so caution is necessary."

"Why aren't the Union soldiers after them?" Mister Ham calls out.

"Too many raiders scattered across the state, I gather," Mister Giles replies. "Besides, these Rebels know the countryside and have allies in every farm and hollow. No soldier from the North is going to track them down."

"Pa could find them," I whisper fiercely.

Old Uncle grunts like he knows it's true, too.

Minutes later, Mister Ham gives a signal and the men follow him down the lane. If I were older, I'd be riding with them.

Frustrated, I kick the trunk of the elm tree, stubbing my still-scabby toe. I hold the throbbing foot while hopping on the other, and I hear Annabelle giggle. I grin at her, glad my pain brought some joy to her morning.

One-legged, I hop up the brick walk to the steps of the veranda. Annabelle's thirteen like me, but in Mistress's hoop skirt she looks close to a woman. I flush. I've grown up with Annabelle, but lately, I've found myself acting something awkward around her. She's a house slave raised in the Main House and I was raised in the stable. There's a world of difference between the two of us. "G-good morning, Miss Annabelle," I finally stammer.

"Why, Gabriel Alexander, when did you get so polite?" she asks.

"I'm just paying my regards," I reply. "I know you've been pining since Mistress Jane passed away."

Her smile fades.

"I'm right sorry," I add quickly. Dropping my injured foot, I leap up two steps, trying not to wince. The blisters I got from Pa's boots—the boots those raiders *stole*—ain't healed yet. "Ma says you've taken it hard."

Her chin bobs. "Mistress Jane was good to me. I don't

31

know what I will do now that she's gone." Annabelle brushes a tear from her cheek. "Gabriel, did you hear that on her deathbed Mistress Jane gave me my freedom?"

"Why, that's grand news!"

"Yes, I suppose it is. But what good does it do me? I know nothing else but this farm. I have no other family. I haven't even been to Lexington, like you have." Her lower lip trembles. "Freedom doesn't mean anything if I'm too afraid to leave."

"Seems you once told me that freedom ain't just about leaving," I remind her. "Might be that if you're patient, the right course will come to you when your heart has healed."

She straightens her shoulders, then gives him a small smile. "Might be," she agrees. "I am impatient sometimes."

"Like me. If I had my way, I'd be off looking for Captain." I try to puff out my chest, which suddenly seems as puny as a banty rooster's. "And if I was a soldier like my pa, I'd be after him like a jackrabbit. But Mister Giles won't allow it. He says my job is to stay here and train Aristo."

Annabelle tilts her head. "Really? I heard it was your *ma* who won't allow you to chase raiders or be a soldier," she declares, suddenly looking like her old self again.

I bristle. "Ma ain't my boss! If I want to chase raiders or join the army, I will, just like that. But first I aim to win more races so I become famous."

"Ooooh. Gabriel, the famous jockey." Annabelle purses her lips, and I know she's mocking me.

"I won on Captain, didn't I?"

"Yes, but then you *lost* him."

32

I grit my teeth. Annabelle is still as pesky as a tick burrowed in my skin.

"Gabriel!" Mister Giles calls from the gateway. He's been jawing with Major Wiley, who stayed behind on his horse. "Come here a moment, please."

"Yes sir." I bid Annabelle a curt good day, then hurry down the walk. Major Wiley is a tough old man with snow-white hair. Some folks say he ain't really a major, but Mister Giles claims he got the title in the state militia.

"Major Wiley would like you to ride two of his Thoroughbreds next week at the Association track."

"You mean jockey them?"

"Yes. I told him that it was fine by me. I won't be racing any horses until the mourning period is over."

"What do you say, Gabriel?" Major Wiley asks.

"Why, I'd be honored, sir!" I toss a triumphant glance toward the veranda, but Annabelle's gone.

"Good. I'd like to try you on Nantura, my three-year-old mare, and Washington, my four-year-old colt. And don't worry, I'll personally escort you to and from the track," the Major adds. "I'm not planning on losing any more horses to those raiders." He tips his hat to Mister Giles. "I need to be off, Winston. Rest assured, we'll find Captain." With a final nod, he spurs his horse and gallops down the lane after the others.

"It looks as if your reputation is growing fast, Gabriel," Mister Giles says. "Major Wiley has good horses and he'll pay you fairly. Now go tend to Aristo. Give him a good workout this morning. I've got big plans for that colt.

Losing Captain won't stop me from winning races."

"Yes sir!" Pleased as a hog in corn, I run up the lane toward the training barn. Before Jackson left, he rode for Major Wiley. Earned good cash, too, as I recall. I grin, already hearing those coins jingling in my pockets. Add them to my fifty dollars, and I'll soon be rich!

Aristo was turned out early this morning. Now he's running across his pasture, acting like a horsefly's after him. I climb the rail fence and whistle to him. The colt trots over, his coat red-gold in the morning sun. Sliding to a halt in the dewy grass, he paws like a wild stallion.

"Best get your wildness out of your system now," I tell him. "'Cause I aim to saddle you this morning."

Aristo hates the saddle. I'd race him bareback, but Mister Giles says Jockey Club rules won't allow it. For weeks, I've been laying sacks and blankets across his back. He don't pay them any mind. But as soon as I set that saddle on his withers and dare to tighten that girth, he blows like a cork from a jug.

Must be some way to fool that horse into loving the saddle.

Pa would know what to do.

Only Pa ain't here, I remind myself once again. Before he enlisted in the army, Pa was the head trainer at Woodville Farm. When he left, Mister Giles hired a trainer from the North named Newcastle. The man was quick with a whip and a nasty word. Lucky for me, he didn't stay long. Now no one's in charge of training, and Mister Giles tells me to use my judgment with Aristo. *Me,* a boy of thirteen.

Sometimes the responsibility feels heavy on my skinny shoulders. But today I feel strong, like I can handle it.

A bee buzzes past and Aristo takes off again. I let him play for a while, enjoying his antics. I'm watching him kick his heels to the sky when the idea comes to me: the colt loves to buck. It's not that he hates the saddle. Throwing the saddle off is just one more excuse to kick up his heels.

I slap my leg. "Why, I'll be a caught possum!" *Listen to the horse,* Pa always told me. If I'd been listening harder to Aristo, I would have figured this out sooner.

Jumping from the rail, I run into the barn and get a rope, a bucket with a handful of feed, and an old racing saddle. Moments later, I slip through the gate into Aristo's pasture. Setting the saddle on the ground behind me, I shake the bucket while calling the colt. He prances over, all excited to see that feed. When he dunks his head in the bucket, I slowly stoop and pick up the saddle. In one swift motion, without a pat or hello, I toss it onto his back and tighten the girth.

The colt explodes. He rears, knocking over the bucket, and charges across the field. When he races back, I vault over the top railing, narrowly missing his flying hooves. He wheels, bucks in place, and then gallops off again.

I raise my eyes to the heavens. "Lord, please don't let the fool horse break a leg."

"Gabriel, what in thunder are you doing?" Cato hollers as he hobbles down the lane from the carriage horse barn. Cato's in charge of the riding and carriage horses. His brother Oliver runs the mare and foal barn.

"Mister Giles told me to saddle that colt," I tell him. "And that's what I did."

Cato cuts his eyes to the Main House like he's scared Mister Giles might show any moment. "Best hope that colt don't crack a hoof or break his wind."

"I'm praying he won't. But I wasn't going to fight that saddle on him—that was Newcastle's way. This way, the colt's fighting himself. And from the looks of it, he's enjoying the battle."

Twisting and leaping, Aristo flies around the pasture. Gradually, his bucking turns into a gallop, then a canter. Finally, he trots towards us, his neck arched, his eyes gleaming. The saddle's tipped on his withers.

Cato shakes his head. "It's a wonder that old saddle stayed on."

"It better. I ain't taking it off his back until the horse feels bare without it."

Cato raises one brow like I'm batty.

I shrug. Might be I have lost my wits. But I don't think so. Aristo lips up the spilled kernels of grain. He's blowing hard, but it seems he's already forgotten the torment perched on his withers.

Beside me, Cato chuckles. "I believe you've got your pa's magic, Gabriel."

"Naw. This was just horse sense. I'm leaving that old saddle on him all night. Then tomorrow I aim to ride him in that saddle. The magic will be sticking to that leather seat while the colt is bucking!"

★★★

After breakfast the next morning, Jase gives me a boost onto the colt. All last night, I left Aristo out in the paddock, saddled up. Now he's acting like he's forgotten it's on his back. Aristo keeps one ear cocked, as if he's thinking about tossing me off. But I stick like a burr to that saddle. Before long I have him trotting around the pasture like one of Mister Giles's riding horses.

The colt's learned to listen to my voice from all the training in the paddock, and he listens to my hands and legs when I work him bareback. Now I'm teaching him to listen with me in the saddle.

If Aristo had his way in a race, he'd gallop full out from start to finish. But a winning horse has to canter easy and save his strength. I need to teach him to listen to my commands so he doesn't burn out in the first heat.

"All right, colt, feel my heel in your right side? Feel my fingers tickling the left rein? That means move left," I tell him. "You need to learn this in case a jockey comes up on your right and tries to bump us into the rail."

With a switch of his tail, Aristo sashays left.

"Now I'm signaling you to move right. Feel it?" I press my left leg into his left side and jiggle the right rein. Arching his neck, Aristo floats to the right, and my heart floats with him.

We practice weaving from side to side at a trot, and then I squeeze him into a canter. The colt's doing fine until he hears the rap of shod hooves coming up the lane. He plants his legs, swivels his head, and stares at the horses approaching in the distance. I recognize Major Wiley and Mister Ham. It's the riders who left yesterday in pursuit of Captain.

I trot Aristo over to the gate. Reaching down from the saddle, I lift the latch and pull it open. As we jog up the lane, I search for a riderless horse among the returning party.

Mister Giles is hurrying from the Main House, a linen napkin tucked in his shirt like he'd been eating his morning meal. We reach the group about the same time. The men are slouched wearily in their saddles, and their horses look jaded.

"Did you find the raiders?" Mister Giles asks. "Any sign of Captain?"

Major Wiley shakes his head. "We rode day and night, following reports that Butler and Keats had joined Sue Mundy's gang and were riding west from Versailles. Tracked them to Bardstown, but they had a head start and our mounts were played out. It appears they're making for the Missouri border."

Taking off his hat, Major Wiley runs his fingers through his white hair. I see defeat in his eyes, and my hopes sink. "I'm sorry, Winston," Major Wiley says solemnly. "Unless the Union troops stationed in Louisville can catch those raiders, your horse is lost for good."

CHAPTER FIVE

aptain's gone and it's *my* cowardly fault. I dare not look at Mister Giles. The other night he said there were worse things than having a horse stolen. To my mind, he's wrong. When Major Wiley recovered his horses from the raiders, two of them were so broken down they had to be shot.

One was Major Wiley's favorite mare, Fancy, who was in foal. Major Wiley begged the raiders not to take her; he told them she'd never keep up. They only laughed. A day later they abandoned Fancy after riding her hard for twenty miles. Pa told me Major Wiley wept like a baby when he pulled the trigger.

I imagine that fate for Captain and my heart goes numb.

"Thank you, men," Mister Giles says. "You did your best. The reward still stands. I won't give up until my horse is found and returned."

Mister Giles heads back to the Main House, his tread heavy on the brick walk. He doesn't even glance at Aristo, so I know his mind is as leaden as his step. It hasn't even been a week since he had to bury his wife, and now this.

I pat Aristo, glad he's safe. When the raiders came to Woodville, One Arm tried to steal him. It was luck and the Union cavalry that saved the colt from Captain's fate.

I'm glad Mister Giles isn't giving up. One day, luck and the cavalry just might save Captain, too.

★★★

The day of the Kentucky Association track meet comes swiftly. I'm jockeying Nantura and Washington, two of Major Wiley's Thoroughbreds. On the long walk to Lexington, I take turns riding both horses, working out strategies for handling them during the race.

Nantura's a heavy-headed, bullish, long-strided mare. She always wants to be in front. The mare hates *anything*—carriage horse, saddle horse, chicken—getting ahead of her. She hates the dirt kicked up in her face and the sight of a tail end. As soon as the race begins, I'll need to get her in front and keep her there.

Washington's a soft-mouthed, skittish, short-strided colt. He rocks when he canters and springs in the air when he sees his own shadow. When I race him, I'll need to stay clear of the other horses and jockeys, coddle him from start to finish, and hope he has enough bounce to end strong.

Major Wiley has kept his promise, and six armed guards flank us, ensuring that our trip to Lexington will be trouble-free. Mister Giles has come along as well. To ease the pain of Mistress Jane's death, I think.

We stop on the main street of Lexington, and Mister

Giles buys me a new pair of riding boots. They're as black and shiny as crows' feathers. I hold them on my lap the last mile of the ride.

When we get to the Association track, which is on the east side of town, Major Wiley waves me away from the barn. "Do what you wish, Gabriel. You're my jockey now. Not my groom."

It's a heady feeling, only I'm too bashful to walk into Lexington with the other jockeys, who'll be drinking, gambling, and boasting about their exploits in the saddle. Instead, I stay and groom Nantura and Washington until their coats are glossy and they know my smell and voice.

Nightfall, I'm too wound up to sleep, so I mosey around the other stalls. By race time, Pa always knew every owner, jockey, and horse at the track. I aim to do the same.

The moon, as round and bright as a china plate, lights my way down the shed row. Despite the hot night, most of the top doors are shut. Finally, at the end of the barn, I find an open door and peer over it.

"Git on outta here," a voice growls from inside. Startled, I stumble backward, colliding with a wooden box. The box and I pitch over and I find myself flat on the ground, looking up at two black faces. Neither is friendly.

"What're you doing snooping around these stalls?" a man wearing a battered felt hat snarls down at me.

"N-n-nothing, sir."

The second man bends at the waist and studies me with squinty eyes. I'm expecting him to spit on me—or worse— when he asks, "Ain't you Isaac Alexander's son?"

I nod vigorously.

"Heck, why didn't you say so?" He holds out his hand and helps me up. "I'm Bates and this is Latham." He introduces the man in the felt hat. "We're old friends of your pa's. How is he? Heard he was fighting Rebels."

"Yes sir, he is." Relieved, I brush off my britches.

"Sorry we was looking at you so suspicious like," Latham says. Lowering his voice he adds, "Rumor has it some scoundrel's sneaking 'round poisonin' the horses."

"Poisoning them? How?" At the track, Pa tended his charges carefully, ever mindful that some owners and trainers will do anything to win.

"Ain't sure, but Master Lewis's horse, Alliance, had something bitter in his grain," Latham explains. "Luckily, the colt only picked at it, so he didn't git sick. Master told us to keep our eyes peeled."

I glance down the shed row. "Is that why all the stall doors are shut?"

"Yup. Everybody's worried 'bout their horses." Bates puts a hand on my shoulder. "Best you not be prowling around tonight. A suspicious groom might whack you with a shovel, thinking you're that scoundrel."

"Thank you for the advice."

I'm turning to go when Bates stops me. "You're jockeying tomorrow, ain't you?" he asks.

"Yes sir. Two of Major Wiley's horses."

"We like the way you ride, Gabriel Alexander," Bates says, and Latham nods in agreement. "And you ain't a slave no more, right?"

"That's right." I straighten my spine. "I'm riding for myself."

Bates steps closer. "We've got a tip for you. Watch out for Alliance's jockey. He's a nasty Tennessee boy. Carries a briar branch up his sleeve."

"Thanks." Usually grooms are fiercely loyal to the horses they care for, so Bates and Latham's tip is an unexpected gift.

"Only thanks we need is you beatin' dat Tennessee boy," Latham says.

"And maybe winning us a little bettin' money," Bates chimes in. "Might be you have a tip for *us?*"

"Put your money on Nantura in the first race," I whisper. "Mare runs to win." I thank them again and hurry toward Major Wiley's stalls. I'm halfway there when I hear a whinny. I stop to listen and hear it again, muffled this time. It's coming from the clearing in the trees where the Negro women cook burgoo, the stew they sell on race day.

This time of night the clearing's dark. Who would be there at this late hour with a horse?

Might be the scoundrel with the poison.

My palms start sweating, and my feet cleave to the ground. Then I hear a smothered snort like someone's clamped a hand over the horse's nostrils. My stomach jumps, and I know I've got to look, despite my chicken-heart. If there is a horse in trouble, I can raise a ruckus and hope that Bates, Latham, and the other grooms will come running.

Stooping low, I run barefoot across the grass to the edge

of the woods. I flatten against a thick tree trunk and cautiously peer around it. In the middle of the clearing I make out the shapes of two men and a horse.

It's too shadowy to see faces, but I can hear voices.

"Two hundred dollars," one man demands.

"Two hundred!" the other scoffs. "Nag ain't worth shucks. I'll give you fifty."

"One hundred fifty. He's a purebred."

"You mean he's pure *lame*. A hundred. That's my top offer."

The two men are horse-trading, I gather. But why at night? There can only be one reason: the horse is stolen, and the men are thieves.

The hair rises on the back of my neck. *Go and get help.* I'm inching away from the tree when I hear the slap of a palm on a flank and the drum of hooves.

"See him trot? Horse ain't so lame."

I freeze. The men are suddenly so close I can smell them.

"Hundred's my final offer. Take it or leave it."

I prick up my ears. The man talks with a Northern accent. Have I heard his voice before?

"I'll take it and be done."

I figure money must be changing hands, 'cause all's quiet except for the horse's breathing.

"And here's twenty more," the man with the Northern accent says. "Twenty Yankee dollars to make sure you leave town and keep your mouth shut."

The other man grunts. Then I hear rustling and a man walks by leading a horse. Stepping back behind the tree, I peek at the man as he passes. He's whip-thin with a bushy moustache.

Newcastle!

Without thinking, I spring from my hiding place. "What're you doing here?" I shout.

Newcastle whirls. One hand goes to his waist like he's got a pistol or knife stuck in his belt. He stares at me like he's trying to recall who I am, then barks out a laugh. "Why, if it ain't Winston Giles's flea-bite of a slave."

"So what're you doing here?" I repeat, furious at seeing the trainer who once whipped Aristo and me. "Mister Giles sent you packing. I saw him put you on the train heading north."

"Must be I got off at the next stop," Newcastle says smugly. "Maybe I decided I was fond of Kentucky and slaves like you to do my bidding."

"I ain't a slave no more."

Newcastle arches one bushy brow. "Don't matter to me. I don't have to answer to no colored boy for no reason. Besides, I have a job here in town. I'm training horses for Doctor Rammer."

The news jerks me upright. *"You're* the trainer he hired from the North?"

"Yup. Man has some high class Thoroughbreds. His mare Rose Girl is entered against Major Wiley's colt." He squirts an arc of chewing tobacco into the trees. "I aim to make sure that Rose Girl has a winning day tomorrow."

"How're you planning on that?" I ask, and then it dawns on me. *"You're* the one who slipped poison into Alliance's feed bucket."

45

Newcastle's face darkens. "Don't be accusing me of nothing you can't prove."

"I can't prove you poisoned the feed, but I can prove you bought that horse off a thief." I point to the horse he's leading.

He sneers. "You know, you've gotten right mouthy since I left. A good beatin' will put you in your place." He raises his hand.

I cower, steeling myself against the blow, and the horse shies away.

Newcastle laughs. "Still a milksop, huh, boy?"

But my attention's on the horse. The colt is brown from ear to hoof. His coat is ashy and his ribs are hollow, but there's something fine and familiar in his clean lines.

Then I draw in a sharp breath. *Captain!*

CHAPTER SIX

Straightening, I stare at the horse. It *can't* be Captain. This colt doesn't have a white star.

"Get away from that horse," Newcastle snaps.

Ignoring him, I step forward and stroke the whirl of hair between the horse's eyes.

"Get away, I said." A strong arm knocks me aside. Newcastle clucks and, shortening the rope, hustles the horse from the circle of trees.

I hold my fingers up to the light of the moon. The tips are black.

"That *is* Captain! You put shoe black on his star!" I shout, hurrying after them.

"*I* didn't," Newcastle wheels to face me. "The two raiders who stole him from you did. Besides, I bought him from that raider fair and square." He chuckles. "And now I aim to get that ree-ward money from Mister Giles. Quite a tidy profit I'll make. I'll concoct some story that'll make me out to be some kind of hero, too."

His smile fades to a sneer as he leans toward me and growls, "And no colored boy's going to get in my way. So don't be running to Mister Giles with your tale. He might believe your word over mine, but no other white man will, so remember that." Thrusting his face even closer to mine, he spits out the last word. I smell his sour breath and my stomach twists.

Without waiting for a reply, Newcastle turns and leads Captain toward the barns.

Tears of anger and frustration rush to my eyes. I know he's right. No other white man will believe my word over his. My being free ain't changed the laws or people's feelings about coloreds.

As I trudge through the moonlight to the barn, I clench and unclench my fists. I tell myself to be content that Captain will soon be home. Despite his lameness and ragged appearance, he should heal fine. And Captain, not my hatred for Newcastle, is what matters most.

★★★

The next morning, I'm in the paddock with Nantura, ready for her race. Major Wiley's groom Peter is holding tight to the mare's reins, trying to keep her from kicking passersby. Peter's stout, but he's just a boy, and it takes all his might to hold the headstrong mare.

Several Jockey Club officials are milling around the paddock, checking the horses entered in the first race. I've already been on the scale. Ninety pounds. Five pounds more than my previous race weeks ago. I've got to tell Ma to go light on the griddlecakes.

I'm ready to mount when I spot Newcastle. He's leading Captain through the crowd outside the paddock. The colt's wet—it rained early this morning—and he ain't been brushed, but someone's rubbed most of the shoe black from his white star.

"Mister Hammond," Newcastle calls to the president of the Jockey Club as he and Captain part the crowd. "I believe you know Mister Winston Giles?"

Mister Hammond hustles toward Newcastle, sputtering, "Excuse me. Excuse me, you can't bring that horse into the paddock. This area is for race entries only."

Whisking off his hat, Newcastle stops. "I'm terribly sorry, sir," he apologizes. "But I have an urgent need to speak to Mister Giles." He nods toward Captain, and I wonder where he's kept the colt hidden all night. "I believe I have found his stolen horse, Captain Conrad."

Newcastle slants a discreet glance at a nearby group of horse owners. Mister Giles is talking with one of the men. That liar Newcastle has known all along exactly where Mister Giles is! All this bowing and scraping is for show.

"You have his horse?" Mister Hammond's blustery expression turns to one of astonishment. By now, most of Kentucky knows about the theft of Captain and the reward. "Why, then," he declares, "we'd better find Mister Giles and let him know right away!"

Mister Hammond weaves around a tall bay horse.

49

"Winston!" he calls, and Mister Giles looks his way. "A man says he has found your stolen Thoroughbred!"

Mister Giles strides over to Mister Hammond, who takes his arm and steers him toward Newcastle. Mister Giles doesn't seem surprised to see Newcastle, so he must have heard the trainer hadn't gone North. But his expression is wary until his eyes light on Captain Conrad.

"By tarnation, it is him!" he exclaims. "Where'd you find him?"

"At some livery on the other side of Lexington." Newcastle launches into such a wild tale that I'm reminded of the traveling magic show that came to Woodville the summer I was ten. Back then the magician tricked us with a sleight of hand. Newcastle's tricking everyone now with a sleight of tongue.

Disgusted, I turn back to Nantura. "I'm ready to mount," I tell Peter, who's staring at Newcastle, open-mouthed. He's under that swindler's spell, as sure as I was under that magician's.

Peter gives me a leg into the saddle and then leads Nantura closer so he can hear the ending of Newcastle's story. I have no choice but to listen, too.

"I recognized the colt immediately from when I worked at Woodville," Newcastle tells all the listeners. "Now I don't know who those men were that had poor Captain," he adds, sincerity dripping like gravy from his lips. "But I believe they were up to no good. I was afraid they'd shoot me, so I told them I'd already alerted the Federals. They ran like scared rabbits."

"Where was this stable?" Mister Giles asks, his expression dubious.

Newcastle scratches his head, as if puzzled. "Danged if I remember. I got lost coming to the track from town last night. I don't know Lexington streets too well, so I stopped at the livery to ask directions. Noticed the owner was acting mighty suspicious." He lowers his voice dramatically, enjoying the attention. "I figured the owner was in cahoots with the Rebels and didn't want no Yankee poking around. It was dumb luck I spied Captain tethered behind the stable—hidden as if they didn't want no one to spot him."

Mister Giles is frowning like he doesn't believe the story, but Hammond claps Newcastle on the back and announces, "Folks, Mister Newcastle here is a brave man who deserves a cheer as well as the reward money."

The crowd roars out a hip, hip, hurrah, and Mister Giles has no choice but to thank the man for finding his horse. "Meet me after the races at the Phoenix Hotel," he tells Newcastle, "and I will have the reward ready for you."

Dropping his chin, Newcastle stares at the hat in his hands. "A reward is not necessary, sir. It was an honor to return your horse."

Mister Giles smiles politely. "Well, that's a lofty sentiment, but I never go back on my word."

"Thank you, sir," Newcastle replies, and I wonder if I'm the only one who sees the smirk beneath his moustache.

Mister Giles takes the colt from Newcastle. At least Captain is in safe hands now. As for that double-tongued

Newcastle, the crowd closes around him, wanting to hear his story again. I can still hear his boasting as they sweep him from the paddock.

I shake my head hard, trying to get rid of all thoughts of Newcastle. I want my mind to be clear for the race. Nantura tosses her mane and prances a bit, and I feel her muscles vibrate beneath me. The mare wants to win, and I aim to do her justice.

"I'm not going to confuse you with instructions on how to ride the mare, Gabriel," Major Wiley says as he hobbles toward us, waving a silver-tipped cane.

"Thank you, sir. The track's sloppy from the morning rain. She'll hate mud kicked in her face, so I aim to keep her in front the way she likes."

The old man nods. "Keep hold of your wits, and good luck."

The bugle blows. Peter leads Nantura from the paddock and onto the track. It's a large field—four colts and three mares—and their hooves make sucking noises in the mud. Ahead of us, the groom Bates walks beside Alliance, who's being ridden by the Tennessee jockey. Nantura jigs past them, splashing up muck, and Bates winks at me.

The first heat of the race is a blur. At the tap of the drum, Nantura breaks fast. I'm so busy holding her steady that I don't look over my shoulder until we flash past the finish-line pole. The nearest horse is five strides behind.

It takes a furlong before I wrestle the mare to a trot. When I turn her around, Major Wiley's laboring up the track toward us. Nantura skitters past, and he reaches for the rein. Concern fills his craggy face. "By golly, that was fast. I hope you left some steam for the last heat!"

"Major Wiley," I pant. "The mare took the bit in her teeth and ran. I just steered her in the right direction and hoped she kept her footing."

Just then the Tennessee jockey trots past us on Alliance. The jockey glares at me, his eyes blue dots in his mud-splattered face. Nantura snaps at Alliance's rump, her teeth barely missing the Major's derby hat.

"Where's Peter?" I need the groom. My arms are tired from holding the mare.

"He's keeping an eye on Washington," Major Wiley replies. "This morning, Judge Davidson found some strange powder in his mare's feed. And Colonel Whitman suspects someone tried to break into his supply stall last night. I'm not taking any chances."

I hold my tongue as I dismount. Now that Newcastle's a big "hero," I don't dare accuse him of something I didn't witness. I walk on Nantura's right while the Major keeps her in check on the left. Together we get the mare to the barn before she can trample any racegoers.

In the second heat, Nantura's just as strong, and we distance the field in the first lap around the track. During the second lap, I hear her breathing harder, so I snug her tight. That's when Alliance closes the gap. He inches up along the inside rail, and as we gallop into the dip, my mouth goes dry. A rider doesn't want to be neck and neck in the dip. Too many things can happen there where the judges can't see you.

I kiss to Nantura, but the sloppy track and breakneck speed have taken their toll on her. From the corner of my left eye, I glimpse a raised arm. Before I can blink, a briar branch slashes through the air, raking my temple, cheek, and ear.

Blood drips into my eyes. I clutch the reins with my right hand. Raising my left, I fend off the next slash. The briar thorns snag in my shirtsleeve, and I jerk my arm across my chest, snapping the branch. It slaps against my left side, stinging the skin beneath my shirt, but it's a niggling pain compared to the fire in my face.

Alliance creeps ahead.

I swipe away the blood, then once again take both reins. I can bear losing because of another jockey's skill, but not because of another jockey's cheating.

I jiggle the left rein. Nantura eyes Alliance, who's ahead by a nose. She pins her ears, furious. I jiggle that rein again, urging the big mare left. She flows toward the inside, forcing Alliance closer to the rail where the dirt's banked and the mud's as sticky as mush.

The colt gets bogged down and Nantura surges past him.

We win by an arm's length. Major Wiley's all smiles when we pose by the judge's stand. I'm grinning, too, although it's hard to tell with the blood pooling in the corners of my eyes and mouth. None of the stewards question the blood, and I don't complain. The Tennessee jockey's trying to win, just like me.

My third win! I think excitedly, marking them with three

raised fingers. Soon I'll have a handful of wins—and a pocketful of riches.

"Masterful riding," Mister Giles calls to me as we pass by the crowd in the grandstand. All his gentlemen friends are smiling, so they must have won big money on Nantura. He points one gloved finger at me. "I have plans for you, Gabriel Alexander. Big plans!"

My chest swells with pride. My name ain't in a newspaper yet, but one day it will be, I know it.

When we get back to the barn, one of the major's grooms takes Nantura. I dismount, wipe off my face and boots, and head to Washington's stall. I need to tell Peter that Nantura's ready for bathing. And I want to talk sweet to that pigeon-hearted Washington, who's entered in the third race. But when I peer over the stall door, I know something's wrong. Washington's in the corner, his head drooping. Peter's nowhere in sight.

"Major!" I holler. "Something's wrong with the colt!"

Major Wiley hobbles over. "Where's Peter? I told that boy not to leave the stall," he fumes as he throws open the door. There's a half-eaten bucket of grain on the floor.

"Dang boy knows not to feed him before the race!" He picks up the bucket to toss it from the stall, but I stop him.

"Check it first," I say urgently.

His face falls as he realizes what I'm suggesting. He holds the bucket up to his nose and sniffs. Then he grabs a few kernels of corn and puts them in his mouth. Immediately he spits them out with a sharp *bah!*

"Sticky and sweet, like some kind of tonic's been poured

on the feed," he says. "Laudanum, probably. Sweet enough so the horse ate it."

I walk over to Washington. Flies buzz around his head and flanks, but he doesn't even swish his tail. I place the flat of my hand under his nostrils. His breath fans my fingers; it's shallow but steady. His eyelids are closed and his lower lip flaps like an old mule's. "He's out cold, but I believe he'll be all right."

Major Wiley sighs heavily. "At least it's not poison. Horse will be too groggy to run. I'll have to scratch him from the race." Rage makes his chin quiver. "Peter was supposed to watch him! Where could that boy be?"

A chill works its way up my spine. Newcastle makes no secret of his dislike for coloreds. Would he hurt Peter?

"Major Wiley, I doubt Peter would leave Washington," I say quickly. "Might be something's happened to him." I bolt past him and head down the passageway. A groom is untacking Nantura. My eyes go to her stall. The door's open wide.

Breaking into a run, I rush down the aisle and into Nantura's stall. Peter's sprawled in the corner, half-covered with straw. My heart thuds against my chest.

I kneel next to him. His lashes lie soft against his light brown cheeks. His chest rises and falls, and my terror drains away. Like Washington, he's only sleeping soundly. His lips are sticky like the corn kernels, and I cast around to find what he ate or drank.

I spy a bottle in the straw under his outstretched arm. Picking it up, I sniff the mouth: applejack. Laced with the drug, too? Ma told me that doses of laudanum were the only thing that brought Mistress Jane peace before she died.

"Peter." I jostle his shoulder, but he sleeps on. *Like the dead,* I think, remembering the time Jase and me found Auntie Wren, Old Uncle's wife, stone cold on the floor of the summer kitchen.

I sit back on my heels, and a heaviness fills me. I'm thankful that Washington and Peter are alive; they'll be fine once they wake up. But for me, the day is ruined. The glory of racing and winning has been tainted by Newcastle's cheating and greed.

CHAPTER SEVEN

I wake on the Sabbath, my legs aching from yesterday's race and the ride back from Lexington. The sun's streaming through the small window, lighting my corner of the cabin. Already it's hot, and I've tossed off the quilt.

Ma must have let me sleep, I think. Grooms and barn workers care for the horses every day. But the horses aren't exercised on Sunday, so a jockey gets that day off.

A fly buzzes against the windowsill, and I hear Ma moving around the cabin. I swing my legs to the plank floor. Next to the bed, my new boots stand stiff and proud like two black soldiers. I bend over and inspect my feet. Not one blister!

A clattering from the kitchen makes me jump from the bed. Mister Giles might let me rest on the Sabbath, but after Bible reading, Ma always has chores for me to do.

As I pull up my britches, I peek around the sacking that hangs from the ceiling, marking off my sleeping area from the kitchen. Ma's bent over by the cupboard, tossing plates and spoons into a basket.

"Morning," I greet her. Last night, I told her all about my adventures at the track. As she listened, she *tsked* and frowned and nodded. Then she hugged me tight, told me I was changing from a child to a man, and sent me to bed.

Ma rises when she hears me, one hand pressed to the small of her back. Her face looks peaked under her headscarf. "Morning, lazyhead. I thought you might sleep the day away." She waves at the table. "Come eat some grits. I brought them from the Main House. Annabelle cooked them. They should still be warm."

"Annabelle?" I wrinkle my nose as I walk over to the wooden table. Ma's set a tin bowl upside down over the plate to keep in the warmth. I tip the bowl up and sniff.

"Mmm. Smells good." I sit at the table, grab a spoon, and dig into the steaming mound. "These grits are right tasty. Are you sure Annabelle cooked them?"

Ma nods. "With buttermilk and bacon grease. Just the way you like."

"Why is Annabelle spending so much time in the kitchen now?" I mumble through a mouthful. "She's never taken much to cooking." Mistress Jane always spoiled Annabelle, which meant the girl only did chores that suited her. And a hot kitchen in the summer was never to her liking.

"Times are hard. Elisa Sue stole away while Mister Giles was at the race in Lexington, and Cook Nancy needs her rest." Ma folds a washrag and tucks it in the basket. "Mister Giles brought in a new girl from the fields to help, but she's just learning."

59

"Might be Elisa Sue left to meet Renny," I suggest.

"Might be. The two did seem sweet on each other." Ma flicks a look at me. "Seems slaves are fleeing the farm every day. Like birds flying north in the spring." She turns abruptly and hurries into the bedroom.

I stop shoveling grits in my mouth. I glance at the basket on the floor—it's filled to the brim—then over to the bedroom doorway. I can hear Ma sniffling softly.

The grits form a lump in my throat. "Ma, what's wrong?"

"I'm leaving, too, Gabriel. Tomorrow." Her voice croaks like a spring peeper. "I'm joining your father at Camp Nelson. Captain Waite, your pa's commanding officer, got me a job as a washerwoman."

The spoon drops from my grasp and clatters on the tin plate as I rise to my feet. "But Ma, you can't leave without me!"

Ma appears in the doorway, her cheeks glistening with tears. "You need to stay here, Gabriel. As much as it grieves me, you must stay at the farm."

My jaw flaps, but no words come out.

"I waited until after the races to decide. I wanted to see if you were ready to be on your own." She smiles proudly over her sadness. "And I believe you are. Not only are you a winning jockey, Gabriel, but you're growing into a fine man."

"Well, I can keep growing at Camp Nelson!"

"No. You'll keep riding here. Keep saving your money. We'll be needing it, all of it." She presses one palm below her waist. I'd almost forgotten that she's with child. Ma's apron and skirt hide the signs.

Crossing the floor, she places her hands gently on my shoulders. I turn my head, unable to look at her. "I wouldn't leave so soon, Gabriel, but I don't want this child born without your pa. Mistress Jane's buried and mourned, and there's nothing holding me at Woodville."

"There's me." Tears rush to my eyes. So much for being a man.

She squeezes my shoulders. "Yes, of course there's you. But you're not a child anymore, and Mister Giles has plans for you." With one finger she tips up my chin. "You want to be a famous jockey, Gabriel. If you leave with me now, you'll never see that dream."

I wipe my tears. "Mister Giles has plans for me?" I vaguely recall him saying some such thing after I raced Nantura.

She smiles, like she has a secret. "He'll tell you about them this afternoon, I think. He's expecting you after Bible reading. Now give me a hug and then help me finish packing."

I open my mouth to protest again, but she hushes me with a finger on my lips. "My mind's made up."

"Can I travel to Camp Nelson with you at least? To see Pa?"

She hesitates. "Only if Mister Giles allows."

"He'll allow it," I declare. "Or I won't go along with his big plans."

Ma laughs at my bold words. "Oh, I'm going to miss you

something powerful, Gabriel Alexander. But I believe you will be right fine without your mama."

★★★

"Come in, Gabriel," Mister Giles calls. He's seated at his desk, his back toward me. He dips a pen in an inkwell and writes on a sheet of paper.

Arms crossed against my chest, I walk into the sitting room and wait until he addresses me. I don't yet know how I will ask him about going to Camp Nelson with Ma. After I helped her get ready for the trip, I checked on Captain Conrad. The colt was contentedly munching hay in his old stall. Tandy was caring for him, so I knew he was in good hands.

Behind me, I hear the swish of skirts and the scuffle of soft-soled shoes on the floorboards. When I glance over my shoulder, I glimpse a shadow rippling along the banister in the hallway.

It's either a haunt or Annabelle.

"Gabriel." Mister Giles suddenly twists in his desk chair.

"Yes sir." I snap to attention.

"That was masterful riding the other day!" Rising from the chair, he paces across the floor. "You were the talk of the meet. Of course, not all the talk was favorable." He lets out a hearty laugh, the first I've heard from him since the mistress died. "But what else would you expect from those who lost bets?"

He picks up the sheet of paper from the desk and waves it. "This is an entry form from the Saratoga Association for their August meet. Think of it! There will be horses from New York, Pennsylvania—even Canada!"

I nod, pretending that I understand. I know the name Saratoga since that's where Jackson went to be a jockey. But I've never heard of those other places.

"Five days of racing!" Mister Giles continues. "There will be the Travers Stakes, the Congress Spring Purse, and the Saratoga Stakes. That famous colt Kentucky will be racing, not to mention Tipperary, Aldebaran, and Fleetwing. Can you imagine? And we're going to be part of it!" He throws his arms wide.

"Part of what, sir?"

"The August meet, of course. I'm entering Aristo, Gabriel. You'll be his jockey. And you'll be riding against Abe Hawkins and Gilpatrick."

My jaw falls slack. *Abe Hawkins? The famous jockey?*

"We leave for Saratoga in five days."

"S-Saratoga?" I stammer. "That's mighty far from Woodville, ain't it?"

"Just think, Gabriel, Aristo will be racing against the finest horses on the finest racecourse in the United States!" Mister Giles's excitement is catching, and my mind starts spinning like a whirligig. In Saratoga I'll get to see Jackson, and I've missed him a lot. Even better, this would be my chance to be famous, just like Abe Hawkins. But then dizziness, or maybe it's fear, comes over me in a rush.

Aristo's mighty fast, but he ain't never been tried on a racetrack. And how could Mister Giles think I'd have a chance against a jockey like Abe Hawkins?

"Sir," I say, my stomach churning. "I don't mean to doubt you, but I've only jockeyed three times. And Aristo's only raced against his stable mates."

Mister Giles waves one hand in the air. "No problem. Tomorrow, we'll try Aristo against Nantura. Major Wiley's already agreed."

"What if Nantura beats him?"

Mister Giles frowns down at me, his fists on his hips. "I thought you had faith in Aristo. I thought you would be excited about Saratoga. This is your chance to prove yourself, Gabriel. To race against the *best.*"

"I am excited, sir. But it's all too large for me. I ain't never been farther than Lexington."

Mister Giles again laughs heartily, like I'm making a joke.

I flush. Maybe Newcastle was right. Maybe I am a milksop.

I lick my lips, which are as dry as cornhusks. "Sir, I would be honored to ride Aristo. But I also want the colt to have the best jockey at Saratoga. And that would be Abe Hawkins. Or what about Jackson? He should be riding in Saratoga by now."

Mister Giles claps me on the back. "Admirable idea, Gabriel, but it's you I want. This trip will be new and frightening for Aristo. We'll be traveling north to New York by train, and the colt will need you every mile of the journey and every furlong of the race."

Traveling north. I repeat Mister Giles's words in my mind. *Jackson said that's where real freedom is.*

"How long will we be gone?" I ask.

"About ten days."

"Can I travel with Ma to Camp Nelson first?" I ask. "I'd like to see Pa."

"Why, of course." Mister Giles rubs his hands together. I haven't seen him this excited in weeks. "Then it's settled! I'll buy train tickets and make the other arrangements. We'll leave Friday."

"Yes sir." I bow slightly at the waist. "And thank you, sir."

As I back out of the sitting room, someone grabs the tail of my shirt and pulls me into the hall. It's Annabelle, and she's glaring at me with pure fury in her eyes.

"Gabriel Alexander!" she hisses as she yanks me into the dining room. "Are you a lack-brain? You have a chance to travel on a train to the *North!* To Saratoga Springs! I've read about that place in the *New York Tribune*. It's a famous resort, and they called it the 'wickedest spot in the United States.' Why, you should be *ecstatic,* not bumbling and downcast."

I snatch my shirt hem from her grasp. Annabelle's always throwing her "learning" in my face like she's better than me. "I don't know what ec…ecst…I don't know what that word means, Annabelle, but I don't care for your bossy tone. You ain't mistress of this house, and I ain't some field slave you can cuss."

Annabelle snaps her chin sideways like I slapped her. Her lower lip quivers, and she bursts into a storm of tears.

Horrified, I step backward, hitting the edge of the mahogany dining table. My elbow bumps a goblet and it crashes to the wooden floor, shattering.

Weeping noisily, Annabelle stoops to pick up the glass.

Her shoulders heave. A shard pricks her palm and blood trickles from the gash. I stare down at her, frozen by her tears and the blood.

"You could help, Gabriel, since *you* broke it," she chides between sobs.

I hunker down, throwing her cautious glances. I know everything about horses, but not one whit about ladies, and Annabelle's tears have me all jangled up. Is she crying because I'm leaving for Saratoga?

"Annabelle, hush," I caution, my voice low as I sweep the glass into a pile. "Mister Giles will hear you."

"So let him hear." Her nose is running and she wipes it with the back of her hand.

I pull a linen napkin from the tabletop and hand it to her. She blows into it, sounding like a mule braying, and I stifle a laugh.

"Oh, you think my tears are funny?" she asks crossly, but I can see she's trying hard not to smile.

"No." I sneak a look down the hall. "They're just noisy. Are you going to tell Mister Giles about the broken goblet?"

"He won't notice." She sighs raggedly. Using the linen napkin, she dabs at the blood on her palm. "He never did care about the running of the house. And it's worse since Mistress Jane died. He eats what's set in front of him. Sleeps in his clothes on the settee. He hasn't set foot upstairs since we buried her. The only thing he thinks and talks about are his precious horses."

Fresh tears trickle down her cheeks, and I know then

that it ain't just my trip to Saratoga that has Annabelle in such a state.

"This house is like a tomb," she goes on. "Like we were all buried with Mistress Jane."

"Hush all this talk of the dead." Standing, I glance nervously around the room. "You'll bring Mistress Jane's ghost back to haunt us."

"Why, I'd welcome that!" Annabelle straightens up. "Least I'd have someone to talk to." Then her anger drains like milk poured from a pitcher and she plops on a dining chair. "Oh, Gabriel, when your ma leaves tomorrow, I won't have *anyone.*"

So this is why Annabelle's so sad. And I can't blame her. I'll miss Ma, too. "You'll have me," I say lamely.

Her eyes flash. *"You'll* be in Saratoga."

I groan. There ain't no way I can keep pace with her moods. "Annabelle, you can read and write and you're *free,*" I tell her. "And Mistress taught you to sing and cross-stitch and curtsy like a lady. Why, you can do anything or go anywhere you want."

Annabelle looks down at her lap. Her fingers pluck at the napkin. "No, I can't. I'm more a stray dog than a lady, Gabriel. I was raised white, but I'm as black as you. There isn't any place for me outside of this farm, this *house.*"

I frown. Is she right? Since I know little about life outside the stables, I can't think of a good answer. "What about going to Lexington to work?"

Annabelle gives an unladylike snort. "I doubt there's much call for a black girl who can cross-stitch and curtsy."

"Well, how about going North?"

"And how would I get there? Mister Giles is all high on buying a ticket for a horse. But I don't see him offering to buy *me* one."

I throw up my hands. "Then make a place here. Use all your big learning to help others."

"Others?"

"Annabelle, you were teaching Ma to read Pa's letters. Why not teach some of the other slaves?"

"Do you think Mister Giles would allow it?"

I shrug. "He ain't going to be here for ten days. You could start while we're gone and see what happens."

She bites her lip. "Would they want to learn?"

I stare at her. Doesn't she know how hungry the slaves outside the house are to read and write? Although I guess I shouldn't be surprised that Annabelle knows so little about the other workers on the farm. Her skin may be black, but she was raised far from the barns and fields. We only know each other because Ma worked in the Main House, too. *"I'd* want to learn," I reply.

Annabelle's lips part in surprise. "You would?"

"I'd like to be able to read Pa's letters, too. Why don't you go down to the quarters one evening and talk to people?" I suggest.

I detect a hint of worry in her eyes.

"Would you go with me? I've never been to the quarters without Mistress Jane or your ma, and that was to visit the new babies and the sick."

"I'd be happy to accompany you."

"I'm much obliged, Gabriel." Annabelle's smile is like sunshine.

"My pleasure." Grinning, I rock back on my heels, feeling less like a milksop and more like a dashing fellow. Might be I *do* know a whit about ladies. But then Annabelle surprises me with a kiss on my cheek. Instantly, my face flames like a torch, my senses fly to the stars, and I realize I know nothing at all.

CHAPTER EIGHT

It takes a whole day to travel to Camp Nelson. Ma's few belongings, some packed in a basket and the rest tied up in a bundle, are stowed in the wagon bed. Pitifully sparse, considering they hold a lifetime. She's left a few things for me back in the cabin, which I'll soon be sharing with Cato and his wife, Taisie. They were moving in their goods as we departed.

Ma's eager to see Pa, and when we get within a mile of the camp she urges the mules to a trot. I'm excited to see Pa, too, but the thought of heading back to Woodville without Ma taints my excitement with sorrow. Fortunately, Mister Giles has allowed Jase to come along, so my return trip won't be so lonely. He's been riding in the wagon bed, but as we approach the gates of the camp, he rises to his knees and stares at the sights.

"Soldiers!" he exclaims. The guards manning the gate are dressed in Union blue. Rifles rest on their shoulders as they march slowly back and forth along the road.

Since I've visited before, I take the reins from Ma and act

like I know what it's all about. "They'll be checking our passes," I say. "Coloreds ain't usually allowed in camp unless they're recruits. It's lucky Captain Waite wrote a letter for you, Ma."

Ma nods primly. She's dressed in lace-up boots, her best frock, and a bonnet instead of a headscarf. *I want to look like a free woman, Gabriel,* she told me. As the soldiers approach, she holds out the letter from Captain Waite. Her head's held high, and I sit tall, too. Pa was promoted to corporal on account of helping Captain Waite catch the Rebel raiders, so we have every right to be proud.

A guard reads the letter, checks our passes, and waves us through the gate. "Refugee tents are on the hill beyond the stables," he tells us.

"I ain't a refugee," Ma corrects him. "I'm to be employed as a laundress."

"Refugee tents are where you'll be staying, ma'am."

Ma purses her lips.

"Ma, you wouldn't want to stay in the Soldiers Home with Pa," I whisper as I crack the reins over the mules' backs. "Men sleep ten deep in a room."

Jase's eyes bug out as the wagon rumbles down the Lexington and Danville Turnpike, which travels right through Camp Nelson. The place is like a town, I tell them, pointing out the bakery, machine shop, and harness shop. "Even has its own hospital and post office," I add, sounding mighty knowledgeable.

I'm looking for the road to the stables when I hear shrill chattering. Six soldiers are herding a group of colored women toward us. The women carry hastily packed bundles. They're barefoot and dirty, and their dresses have scandalously low-cut necks, showing too much flesh.

The woman leading the group is as black and flinty as iron. Her jaw's moving and her hands are waving as she berates the soldiers with every step. When she sees our wagon, she halts.

"Keep moving," the soldier on her right barks.

The woman ignores him. "Why is *that* colored woman allowed in here?" Her arm is raised and one stiff finger points at Ma. "Why are we being thrown out and *those* Negroes are coming in?"

"We've got our orders. Keep moving." The soldier prods her with the butt of his rifle. Pressed on by the others, the woman reluctantly walks past us. When she gets close enough, she spits on the ground under our wheels. "May the devil Speed S. Fry heap his curses upon you all," she cusses as we roll by.

I flush and slap the reins on the mules' backs. As we turn right and head up the hill toward the stables, the only sound is the creak and rattle of the wagon. Finally Jase breaks the silence. "Is Speed S. Fry really the devil's name?"

"No, Jase. He's a brigadier general," I explain. "He's the one who wrote a letter so Jackson and me could visit Pa earlier. He's the officer in charge of the whole camp."

"Then why's that lady cussing him?"

"That wasn't no lady," Ma says huffily.

I flick my eyes at Ma, who's glaring straight ahead. "I

reckon they cussed him 'cause he's the officer who ordered them thrown out."

"Why're the soldiers throwin' them out?" Jase persists.

Ma sets her lips even tighter.

"Might be because unmarried women aren't allowed," I say, throwing Jase a frown that says *hush your questions.*

When we reach the stables, I halt the mules in front of a hitching post. The stable area consists of four long barns arranged like the sides of a box. A large fenced pen has been erected in the middle of the stable yard. Hoots and hollers are coming from the enclosure, and I stand up to see what the noise is all about.

Colored soldiers wearing dusty uniforms are scattered around the pen. Each has a horse wearing a halter and tethered by a lead rope. Saddles sit on the top rails, and some soldiers have blankets in hand. It appears they're attempting to saddle their mounts. The horses circle, rear, and buck in protest.

"Jase, get up here." I gesture for him to join us on the wagon seat. "You gotta see this."

We watch a soldier throw a blanket on a sickle-hocked bay. The horse humps his back, and the blanket slides under his legs, scaring the tar out of him. Yanking the rope from the soldier's grasp, the horse careens across the pen.

"I can handle a horse better than that," Jase says.

A tall soldier with a corporal's stripe calmly chases down the loose horse. Reaching up, he pats the horse's neck, and I see that it's Pa.

"Ma, look. There's Pa! He must be in charge of all these soldiers."

I wave my arm. "Pa!"

He spots us. For a second, he stares like he can't believe his eyes, then his face breaks out in a grin. "At ease, men," he orders. "Praise your horses and walk them quietly. Let them smell the saddles and blankets. We'll try again later."

Still smiling, he strides across the pen. "Lucy! Gabriel! What are you doing here?"

"Didn't you get my letter?" Ma asks.

He shakes his head. His face is dusty but it shines with love. In one swift move, he vaults the fence. Reaching his arms high, he beckons for Ma to climb down from the wagon. Her smile's as big as his, and when she jumps into his arms, he wraps them tightly around her.

Then he gestures for me. "Get down here, boy." I spring from the wagon, and he clasps me to his side with one arm. A moment later, Jase joins the hug.

"Mail's slow here," he tells Ma. "But it don't matter. I'm delighted to see you. It's been too long, Lucy." Dipping his head, he kisses her.

Heat rises up my neck, and it ain't from the sun. Jase giggles behind his hand and a chorus of whistles rings from the pen.

"Whoo-eee, that's what I call being in command!" one of the soldiers hollers.

Pa breaks off the kiss. Ma's holding onto her bonnet and grinning, all flustered. I've never seen Ma and Pa act so foolish. I'm relieved when Pa tells us to wait for him by the wagon.

"I'm almost finished with my men," he says. "Then I'll escort you to your tent."

"Almost finished?" I eye the soldiers and horses in the pen. "Ain't but two horses wearing saddles out of the whole bunch."

Pa sighs. "I know. I sure could use you and Jase for a week, Gabriel. You could help me break these horses."

"Are you organizing a cavalry, Pa?" I ask excitedly.

"Might be. General Burbridge is asking for the authority to organize a colored cavalry regiment."

"That's grand!" I exclaim. "And Pa, you know horses better than any soldier. Why, they should put *you* in command."

"Well, I doubt that, but I am helping Captain Waite prepare. And it's a job, that's for sure. We've seized a hundred horses from disloyal Kentucky citizens." He nods at the animals in the pen. "White soldiers picked over all the good mounts. Colored soldiers got the carriage and plow horses—and a few young ones that ain't broke." He waves his hand at the men in the enclosure. "And my future cavalry soldiers? They're field slaves who ain't never put a foot in a stirrup iron."

"Isaac," Ma says, "organizing these men into a cavalry is likely to be one impossible task."

He grins. "You sound like the white soldiers who mock us every chance they get. But I aim to help turn this ragtag lot into the finest mounted regiment in the United States Army."

"And I aim to join them," I declare.

"Me, too," Jase pipes up.

I thrust out my chest. "Now that the Union army's organizing a colored cavalry, there ain't nothing to stop me."

"Me neither!" Jase puffs out his chest, too.

Ma arches one brow under her bonnet. "My, someone must have forgotten Mister Giles's plan for him to ride racehorses at Saratoga."

Pa tips back his kepi. "Saratoga! Why, you'll be riding with Abe Hawkins, son. Ain't no reason to pass that up."

"Fighting for freedom is reason," I declare.

"For freedom!" Jase echoes.

Pa crosses his arms and aims a stern eye at Jase, then at me. "I want your name in the paper 'cause you won a famous race, Gabriel. Not on the list of dead found on the battlefield."

I drop my gaze. "Yes sir."

"Go to Saratoga. See something of the country." He tousles my hair and then gives Ma a quick peck on the cheek before heading through the gate into the enclosure. I climb on the bottom rail and watch him stride into the middle of the pen. His voice booms out a command, and the soldiers quickly form a line, their horses standing smartly by their right shoulders.

They respect Pa, and so must I, I think. I do want to jockey Aristo, but every time I come to Camp Nelson and see the

colored soldiers, a spark flares in me and I want to be training and drilling.

"You and me'll enlist one day, ain't that right, Gabriel?"
Jase asks. He's leaning his arms on the top rail, too, watching with the same hungry look in his eye. I just nod.

When Pa is done for the day, Jase and me unhitch the
mules. Pa shows us where to bed them down for the night
and where to leave the wagon. Then he slings Ma's bundle
over his shoulder and leads the way to the refugee camp.

I carry the basket, which bumps my leg as I walk beside
Pa, trying to match his stride. Jase walks beside me, and we
chant *left…right…left…right,* pretending we're soldiers
marching off to war.

"Company…halt!" I order when I spot the refugee
camp. The camp's nothing more than two rows of dirty
white tents with a lane in between—like buildings lined up
on both sides of a city road. Except here there's no packed
earth, no cobblestones, no brick walkway. Just mud.

"Pigs sure would love wallowing here," Jase says.

"Company for*ward,*" I order. Slogging through the mud,
Jase and me catch up to Pa, who's stopped in front of one
of the tents. He pulls back the flap and, with an exagger-
ated bow, waves Ma inside.

The tent has a straw floor, tamped and gritty. In one
corner a wooden box serves as a table. In the other corner,
two rumpled and stained quilts cover a mound of straw.
Despite the sparse furnishings, it looks recently lived in. I
wonder if it was once the home of the iron-faced lady.

"This is where your ma's going to live?" Jase whispers

to me. His straw bed in the barn must look fine in comparison.

"Why, it just needs a little tidying up!" Ma exclaims with false cheeriness.

Pa snatches up the dirty quilts. He won't look her in the eye, so I know he's ashamed of what he and the camp can offer. "We'll clean out the old straw and put in fresh, Lucy. We'll lime the ground and chase out the bedbugs. And I can rustle up another box and perhaps a chair. You won't have to share the tent, neither. Colonel Waite promised me."

Ma smiles reassuringly. "Isaac, there ain't no need to fret. Can't be any worse than the soldiers' quarters. 'Sides, I'd stay no matter." With a sigh, she steps into his arms.

Hastily I drop the basket on the ground, and Jase and me rush from the tent, dropping the flap behind us. "Whew. That's more kissing than I care to see ever again," Jase says.

We mosey down the lane between the two rows of tents. There are colored folks everywhere, mostly women and children, but several old men, too, who sit on upturned boxes, watching us pass with clouded eyes.

"You boys got a coin to spare?" one asks.

Another man holds out a whistle he's whittled. His threadbare shirt is held together by one button.

"I ain't got any money to pay you for it," I tell him.

He nods at my shirt. "I'll take that. To chase the damp from my bones."

I swallow. Life for free blacks sure seems hard. Jase pushes me from behind and we run to the end of the tents. A circle of iron tubs steams over fires. Beyond the fires, wash lines draped with long johns and socks stretch from tree to tree. A dozen women huddle over the boiling tubs, stirring with long wooden sticks. A pile of dirty clothes is heaped beside each tub.

One of the women peers at us through the steam. She's a girl, not much older than Annabelle, but she's stooped like an old woman, as if the endless laundry has bowed her back.

"This must be where your ma's going to work," Jase says.

I nod, my eyes on the girl. Her face and hands are red and swollen from the steam and the lye. My heart grows as heavy as the boiling clothes. Is this freedom? Washing soldiers' dirty long johns? I want to run back to the tent and tell Ma to come home to Woodville with me.

But I don't lift my feet from the mud, because I know that this is where Ma has chosen to be. With Pa. From now on, the rows of tents and steaming tubs, not Woodville farm, will be her home.

CHAPTER NINE

Whooo, *whooo.* The shrill train whistle jerks me from a dreamless sleep. I bolt upright, instinctively checking on Aristo. The colt's head hangs above me over the wooden door of the stall in the train's freight car. When he sees I'm awake, he strikes the back wall with his iron-shod hoof.

"Quit that," I warn. Feeling sour, I lean back on my blanket and stare up at Aristo. After he soundly beat Nantura in the match race at Major Wiley's farm, there was no doubt the colt could win a real race on a track. But it's a long journey to Saratoga, and Aristo's been restless since we left a day ago. The train conductor's already been back three times to complain about the colt's kicking. But I can't blame him: I'm pining mightily for Woodville Farm, too. It'll be a wonder if we survive this train journey, much less win a race.

Aristo bobs his head, trying to get my attention. When I ignore him, he snorts and pushes my shoulder with his nose.

"Dang it, horse. I ain't your handkerchief." Hopping up, I toss a handful of hay into his stall and feed him a carrot. I wisely brought a sack full that Annabelle helped me dig from the kitchen garden. Carrots held out in front and two men holding crossed ropes behind his rump were the only way we got him in the freight car.

I stroke his sweaty neck. The car's hot, and flies settle on his rump. He pins his ears and stomps a hoof.

"Shhh." My body sways to the rhythm of the wheels on the track. "It'll only be a while longer."

A whole night and day longer, but I don't mention that. Aristo ain't used to being cooped up. Since we left, he's been locked in one of the narrow stalls built in a corner of the freight car. The conductor told me the other three would soon be filled with horses. "Don't get too comfortable," he'd said.

Fat chance anyone could be comfortable in here. The floor is hard, and the other stalls stink of urine-soaked straw and rotted manure. Before loading Aristo, we cleaned out his stall, limed it, and put down fresh straw. The extra work held up the train, but it was worth the trouble. Mister Giles ran back and forth along the track, pressing silver coins in the palms of the station master, engineer, brakemen, and conductors, so they, at least, were happy to oblige. The passengers weren't quite as forgiving.

Clackety-clackety-clackety... The noise of the train is constant, reminding me of the drone of cicadas. The freight car door's slid halfway open and I peer out. Last night, when Mister Giles checked on us, he told us we were in

Columbus. "That's in Ohio," he explained, "the state north of Kentucky."

I look out at this place called North, but the countryside flashes by too quickly to take it all in. So far, Ohio looks a lot like Kentucky. Farms, small towns, trees, and fields. Disappointment sticks in my craw. Somehow, I thought North would be different.

Whooo...whoo. Again, the whistle signals that the train's approaching a station. Overhead, I hear the thudding of feet as a brakeman runs along the roof of the car to reach the brake wheel.

Clackety, clack-e-ty, clack...e...ty... The rhythm slows. I force the door open wider and let the air blow on Aristo. He whinnies loudly, as if hoping another horse will answer.

With a whoosh of steam and the clanking of couplings, the train pulls into the station. I grab Aristo's empty bucket. The stifling heat makes the horse thirsty, and I fetch water for him at every station.

When the train stops, I jump from the car. Passengers are streaming onto the station platform. There's a sign saying what town we're in, and I wish Annabelle were here to read it. I glance toward the locomotive, spotting a water pump.

I hurry down the platform, dodging passengers exiting the cars. Pumping the handle, I fill the bucket and then head back, walking around the cowcatcher sticking out from the nose of the locomotive to the far side of the train so I don't jostle into the departing passengers. Smoke and steam hiss from the smokestack, and I wave to the engineer with my free hand.

Slowly, I make my way down another track that runs along the other side of the train. Water slops from the bucket onto my bare feet. Two girls with saucy velvet caps and blond curls peer down at me from the window of a passenger car. "Hey, you, colored boy!" one calls. When I look up, she tosses me a licorice twist.

I thank her with a grin and tuck it in my pocket. As I approach the freight car, I hear yelling and the *rat-tat-tat* of hooves. My pulse quickens. *Aristo!*

I set the bucket down and clamber over the coupling. A group of men are trying to load two horses—a chestnut and a bay—onto the freight car. My heart quiets and I wipe my brow with relief. *Not* Aristo.

The chestnut is standing at the bottom of the ramp. His legs are stiff, his eyes roll, and his hooves are planted firmly. Halfway above him on the ramp, two men tug on the lead rope. Their faces are bright red from the strain. I'd like to tell them that no matter how hard they yank, they ain't strong enough to pull that horse up the ramp. And by the looks of that horse, he ain't going to budge.

A man in a tweed suit, vest, and bowler hat watches from the platform. He has sharp eyes and a mustache that curls in a smile. A fat cigar pokes from his mouth. "I don't have time for this. Get the whip, Hooks," he tells a tall boy who hovers at the end of the ramp.

"Yes, Mister Jeremiah," Hooks replies as he scurries to a trunk.

I wince, hating to see any animal whipped. There's a better way to load a horse. But do I dare speak?

Mind your own business, I warn myself. Turning, I retrieve the bucket of water and maneuver it over the coupling. Hooks is behind the horse, flicking its hind legs with the whip. Terrified, the horse rears so high that it falls over, and several ladies on the platform scream.

The horse scrambles to its feet. There's a gash on its hock. A lady swoons, and a little girl starts crying.

"Go easy, Hooks!" Jeremiah growls after glancing at the gathering crowd. "Faraway needs to be fit to race."

Hooks nods. He's getting ready to strike the horse again when the freight conductor bustles over. "Mister Jeremiah, we cannot have you beating your horse in front of the ladies and children."

Mister Jeremiah pulls his cigar from his mouth. "And what would you suggest I do? Carry him up the ramp like a suitcase?"

"Well, I-I..." The freight conductor casts around as if searching for an answer. I look around, too, hoping to see Mister Giles. Mister Jeremiah is obviously an owner taking his horses to Saratoga, too. Mister Giles would be able to reason with him, but I doubt he's left his private seat in the gentlemen's car.

"I don't know how you'll load those animals," the conductor says. "But if you don't get it done in"—he checks his watch—"fifteen minutes, the train is pulling out."

Setting down the bucket, I step onto the platform. The

crowd is growing bigger, like they ain't got anything better to do than watch. "Excuse me, sir." I address Mister Jeremiah in my politest voice.

He looks down at me with clear annoyance. Plucking the cigar from his mouth, he blows out a cloud of smoke. "Go away, kid. I don't give money to street urchins."

"Sir, I'm the...uh...*groom,* for Mister Winston Giles's horse, Aristo, and I can help you load that chestnut colt."

Jeremiah scowls and sticks the cigar back in his mouth. "Winston Giles?" he repeats, the cigar wagging like a dog's tail. "Never heard of him. But if you can get that horse in the car, I'll give you a silver dollar."

"No need to pay me, sir. Just have your boy Hooks put the whip away."

He gestures with his cigar for Hooks to get out of the way. I run up the ramp and grab my carrots and the long ropes. It takes me a while, but I soon have a rope tied on each side of the freight car door. I explain to the two men how to stand at the bottom of the ramp, making a lane with the ropes. I lead the horse to the end of the ramp and tell the men to switch sides, crossing the ropes behind the horse's rump as they go. "Stand far enough away so the colt can't kick you. Now, slowly walk toward the freight car, keepin' the rope taut above his hocks."

The two men oblige and I stand on the ramp with the horse's lead rope. By now the colt has calmed. I feed him a bite of carrot, then back slowly up the ramp. The chestnut takes a step, retreating when the ramp clanks.

From inside the car, Aristo whinnies. The chestnut

pricks his ears. I wave the carrot and the two men press the ropes against the horse's hind legs so it can't move backwards.

I hold out the carrot, talk sweet, and wait patiently for that horse to make up his mind to load. After a spell, Mister Jeremiah frowns and checks his watch. Hooks scowls and taps the whip against his leg. The baggage handlers are loading the last trunk onto the baggage car.

The sun's beating down, and sweat beads on my brow.

Finally, Mister Jeremiah puts his watch away. He shakes his head in disgust and flaps his hand at Hooks as if to say, "Time for the whip."

"Come on, horse," I whisper. "Or they'll hit you again."

"All aboard!" the conductor hollers.

Aristo whinnies a second time. "Come on," I cajole in my prettiest voice as Hooks steps behind the horse. Suddenly, with a bob of his head, Faraway strides up the ramp and into the freight car.

Cheers erupt from the crowd.

Thank you, Lord, I pray silently. Hooks leaps up the ramp, and without so much as a thank-you, snatches the lead rope from me. He backs Faraway into the stall opposite Aristo. Using the same method, we quickly load Senator, the bay horse.

I roll up my ropes and carry my bucket into the freight car. While Aristo drinks, two men remove the ramp. Hooks and a second fellow throw a valise, an empty bucket, and a small trunk through the door. The whistle blows, warning everyone that the train is departing.

The train starts moving. At the last second, Hooks vaults into the freight car. Reaching down, he grabs the other fellow's hand. "Hurry up, Cuffy," he snaps. As the train picks up speed, Cuffy trots beside the car, a scared expression on his face. I'm thinking he ain't going to make it when Hooks hauls him into the car.

Cuffy claps Hooks on the back. As the two shove their luggage and supplies into the middle of the car, they don't even grace me with a look.

I sit down on the blanket, my back against Aristo's stall door. He's contentedly munching hay, happier now that he's got other horses for company.

Hooks pulls a deck of cards from his back pocket. He sits on the trunk, Cuffy leans back on the valise, and they begin to play poker.

I watch them as they toss pennies in a growing pile and raise the stakes. I had them pegged as grooms, although now I have my doubts. They haven't paid a whit of attention to the horses. Plus, they're white. That alone makes me mighty curious. I've never seen a white groom before. White trainers and white jockeys, yes, but in Kentucky all the grooms I've seen are slaves.

I check out their clothes. They're both wearing blue denim pants and leather brogans, and my homespun britches and bare feet suddenly embarrass me. Seems that workers in the North dress in style.

Hooks shoots a suspicious look at me. "What are you staring at, darky?"

Startled, I avert my eyes. "Nothin'."

Hooks bounces off his seat on the trunk. Swift as a cat, he grabs my shirt collar and yanks me to my feet. "You think you're better than me?" he hisses. "Just 'cause you got that horse loaded?"

Speechless, I shake my head. He's a foot taller and a good fifty pounds heavier than I am.

Behind us, Cuffy chuckles.

"Or maybe you're thinkin' you'll ask Mister Jeremiah for my job?" He tightens his grip, cutting off my air. I scrabble at his hand on my collar, trying to loosen his fingers. He only tightens it more, like a noose.

"Well, don't even *think* it." His face is inches from mine and spittle sprays my cheek. "'Cause if you do, this is what's goin' to happen." With a jerk, he drags me across the floor and thrusts me into the open doorway of the freight car.

I grab onto the door frame, bracing myself. The air slaps my cheeks. My fingers cramp. He shakes me hard, and my grip on the doorframe weakens.

"Got the message?" Hooks growls.

I can barely nod. He lets me go, and for an instant I'm suspended in air, my shirt billowing. The ground rushes beneath me as the wind tries to pluck me from the freight car.

CHAPTER TEN

Straining hard, I drag myself from the buffeting wind and back into the car. Gasping, I lean against the wall.

Hooks is sitting on the trunk, fanning out his cards as if nothing happened. Cuffy's still chuckling to himself.

I rub my throat. It's raw and bruised from the strangling collar. Worse, my hopes are raw and bruised as the realization hits me: *The North ain't any different.*

I should have known it. Newcastle was from the North, and he's about as no-account as they come.

Blinking, I fight back the rising tears. I refuse to let a Northerner see me cry.

That night I sleep in Aristo's stall, pressed in the front corner. I feel safer next to the colt's iron-shod hooves than in the open freight car.

When I wake, sunlight's streaming through the doorway of the car. I rise, stretch stiffly, and give Aristo's flank a pat. The outside air feels fresh and crisp, but it can't mask the rank smell of the dirty stalls.

Ducking under Aristo's neck, I peer over his door. Hooks and Cuffy are passed out on the floor. Several empty bottles roll between them. Last night they jumped from the train at several stops to buy cheap whiskey. Never once did they bring water to their horses or check the gash on Faraway's leg.

I touch the bruises on my neck, wondering if I dare give their horses a drink. I don't fancy getting tossed off the train, and according to Mister Giles, Saratoga Springs will be the first stop this morning. The horses might be able to wait until then.

I don't know if I can wait, though. The stop will be none too soon for me.

I bundle up my blanket, unlatch Aristo's stall door, and slip through. I ready my few things, tying them into my blanket. Then I feed and water Aristo and brush him until his coat shines like copper. When he steps off the train, everyone in Saratoga will note the arrival of the greatest horse in Kentucky.

Quietly I step from the stall and around Hooks's legs. There's half a bucket of water left, and I offer it to Aristo. But the colt must know that the journey's coming to an end. Ignoring the water, he stares out the door, his mane ruffling in the wind.

I look, too. We've left farmland behind, and all I can see are trees, which cover the rolling hills like green quilts on a lumpy mattress. The forest is so thick that it's hard to picture a town like Saratoga nestled in one of the valleys.

When I turn back, Hooks and Cuffy haven't stirred.

Stepping over Hooks, I give Faraway and Senator the rest of the water. Senator sucks the bucket almost dry, then noisily slurps the few drops at the bottom. Hooks groans like he's waking, and I scuttle back to Aristo's stall.

I press my back against the door. Clutching the bucket, I stare down at Hooks and decide that I'll crack his head with it if I need to.

Hooks yawns and sits up, but he's so slow moving and bleary eyed that I decide he's not much of a threat. I set the bucket by my feet and pull Aristo's halter from a hook on the door. Cuffy keeps on snoring, even when the whistle blows and the brakeman runs overhead. As I slip the halter onto Aristo, my heart starts pattering. *We're finally here!*

"Get up." Hooks prods Cuffy with the toe of his shoe. "Get up, or Jeremiah will know we've been drinking."

Cuffy groans. Hooks throws the bottles out the door, and they shatter on the gravel beside the track. Then he stands, sways to get his balance, and aims a hard kick at Cuffy's ribs.

With a howl, Cuffy pops upright. "What'd ya do that for?"

"Look smart. We're pulling into the station."

The train hisses as it slows. I stick my head out the door and watch the cars ahead wind up the tracks through a deep cut in the tree-covered hills. Then the trees grow sparse, revealing dirt lanes and white clapboard cottages. Gradually, the lanes change to roads and the clapboard cottages give way to two-story buildings.

Down the track, I glimpse the Saratoga Springs station.

Horse-drawn vehicles surround the station: swift rock-aways, fringed surreys, and sturdy coaches. As the train draws near, a swarm of drivers hurries onto the platform.

When the train stops, the conductor shouts, "Saratoga Springs—twenty minutes for breakfast!" Passengers pour from the train. Everyone's arriving for the racing meet, I gather.

Hooks and Cuffy toss their baggage to the ground and jump off after it. Freight handlers secure the ramp, dropping it with a clank. Aristo impatiently raps the stall door with his front hoof.

I scratch his forehead. "Easy does it, colt." But like me, he's had his fill of this ride.

Two men unload Faraway and Senator. Aristo whinnies after them. I peer up and down the bustling platform. There's no sign of Mister Giles.

Buggies filled with passengers, satchels, and trunks begin to leave the station. As I watch them drive away, panic churns in my stomach. I'm about to go down the ramp when I spy Mister Giles approaching along the platform. A hunched-over man in a snuff-colored overcoat hobbles beside him. Behind them, a baggage handler pushes a hand-cart stacked with luggage, the racing saddle teetering on top.

"Gabriel!" Mister Giles waves his cane at me. "How was the last leg of your journey?"

"Fine sir," I call, "but I'd like permission to unload Aristo. Neither of us is interested in traveling to the next stop."

"Permission granted, although there's no chance of the train leaving with you on board," Mister Giles assures me. "The engineer was handsomely bribed. I had to find Mister Baker here before I could come for you."

I duck back into the car and hurriedly open Aristo's stall door. Aristo clatters down the ramp, pulling me with him. When my feet hit firm ground, I breathe easier.

It's then that I spy a small boy, half-hidden by the tower of luggage on the handcart. The boy looks to be about Jase's age, but inches shorter. A porkpie hat sits flat on his tangled blond hair. Under the upturned brim, his blue eyes peer from a skinny face dotted with greenish-yellow bruises. His knee-length britches are patched, and his shirt is so small that the buttons strain to stay fastened.

"What do you think, Baker?" Mister Giles asks, gesturing toward Aristo. Hooking his thumbs in his lapels, the hunched-over man inspects the colt with an appraising eye.

Head high, neck arched, Aristo whirls on the end of the rope, staring at the unfamiliar sights. The sun gleams off his golden brown coat; his tail streams behind him like a silken flag. Except for his dirty leg wraps, the colt looks perfect.

"You have yourself a fine horse," Mister Baker finally replies.

"Thank you, sir. Major Wiley spoke highly of your stable, so I trust my horse will be in good hands."

"I only await your orders. *Short Bit!*" the man barks so suddenly that I jump. The boy darts around Mister Baker like his raggedy britches are on fire. "Hop into that freight car and get the supplies. Mister Giles's boy here will help you."

Short Bit scoots up the ramp, and after handing the rope to Mister Giles, I follow. Behind me, I hear Mister Giles say, "Gabriel is Aristo's jockey. He's young and inexperienced, but he's got hands of velvet and nerves of iron."

Ears burning, I stoop to retrieve my blanket-wrapped bundle and the bucket of brushes. Short Bit picks up the water bucket. He's mouse quiet, and his eyes follow me like he's never seen a colored boy before. Lifting the half-empty feed sack with one arm, he flings it over his shoulder, staggering under the weight.

"I'll carry that." I hold out my hand.

He tenses and backs away, not taking his eyes off me—like he's afraid I'm going to ball my hand into a fist and add to his bruises. When his bare heels hit the ramp, he spins and runs down.

I frown. The boy's white, yet he acts like a whipped slave.

I check to make sure we have everything and then go down after him. Mister Baker and Mister Giles are leading Aristo to a carriage parked next to the station. Short Bit trots after them, bent like a branch under the weight of the sack.

The train blows its whistle. I glance over my shoulder and watch it slowly pull away. I sure ain't sad to see it go. Yet I can't help but smile, 'cause the next time I board that freight car, I'll be a famous jockey.

The baggage handler helps us load the carriage. Mister

Baker drives the team while Short Bit and me walk behind, leading Aristo. I'm so bug-eyed at the sights that I'm glad Short Bit is along. He hasn't said a word and he barely reaches Aristo's neck, but he knows how to calm the colt when I'm distracted.

And Saratoga has *lots* of distractions.

To be sure, the town ain't as big as Lexington. But it looks to be geared for one thing: pleasuring visitors. Stores and shops line the streets, offering fancy goods I ain't never seen before. A brass band toots a lively tune on a street corner. A juggler wearing an advertising banner like a cloak walks in the middle of the road, maneuvering around the stream of carriages. "Come see the two-headed nightingale and the tiny Italian dwarfs," he calls as he tosses red balls in the air.

A lady struts past, her face painted with bright hues. She's covered with yellow feathers from her neck to her ankles. "Arriving tonight at the Music Hall," she announces as she passes out handbills, "Madame Caroline, the songbird from New York City."

"This is Broadway," Mister Baker tells Mister Giles as the carriage turns right. "Saratoga's main thoroughfare."

Broadway is as wide as a river and lined with towering elm trees. It's crowded with coaches, buggies, strolling visitors, and fancy-goods stores. But what's really eye-popping is the huge hotels. They're four and five stories tall. Marble stairs lead to their white-columned verandas, called piazzas, which stretch along Broadway for as far as I can see. On the piazzas, ladies and gentlemen sit in high-backed chairs and rockers, reading, talking, playing cards, sipping drinks, and smoking.

This must be what Jackson was talking about. I look across the crowd, hoping to spot him. He never let us know if he made it to Saratoga, but if he did I sure hope I can find him.

"To your left is Music Hall," Mister Baker points out as we travel slowly down Broadway. "To your right are the United States Hotel, the American Hotel, and the Grand Union Hotel."

We journey several blocks, the dust from hooves and wheels swirling about our heads. With each step, Aristo trembles with excitement. Too wrought up to walk, he prances by my side, his ears swiveling like ladies' fans.

"On your left is Congress Hall, where you'll be staying," Mister Baker tells Mister Giles. "It's one of the finest hotels in Saratoga. Across from it is the Congress Springs. Saratoga is noted for its healing waters, Mister Giles. I hope you'll partake while you're here."

Beyond Congress Hall, on the other side of Broadway, is a gash of blackened buildings. Aristo snorts at the smoky smell wafting our way.

"Had a fire not too long ago." Mister Baker shakes his head. "Started by the Fourth of July fireworks."

The carriage makes a left turn, barely missing a dray wagon hauling wood. "This is East Congress Street," Mister Baker says. "About a mile up and to your left is the old Trotting Course. Stabling facilities are located there. Across the street is the new racecourse."

"How convenient," Mister Giles says. "Before we go any

farther, I'd like to buy Gabriel something to eat. I need my jockey to stay hale and hearty."

"By all means. I'll have my boy buy him something." Mister Baker stops the carriage in front of a saloon and hollers, *"Short Bit!"*

Short Bit dashes to the side of the carriage, and Mister Giles tosses him a coin. Then he disappears around the rear of the saloon, one hand holding his porkpie hat. I'm circling Aristo, trying to keep him off my toes, when the boy careens back around the corner and hands me something wrapped in brown paper.

"Thanks." I sniff the package. It smells pungent and fishy. My mouth waters. I'd been so busy looking at the sights, I'd forgotten about breakfast.

Short Bit takes Aristo's rope from me. As we head up East Congress, I unfold the paper, revealing two slices of brown bread. Gray, slimy things poke from between the slices.

I wrinkle my nose. "Smells like heaven, but looks like something a cow left behind."

Short Bit licks his lips. "Oysters," he breathes, as if he's dreaming of a sandwich of his own. At least I know he's not mute.

I've heard of oysters, but I've never eaten one. Opening wide, I bite into the greasy mess. I chew warily, swallow, and sigh with pleasure. Short Bit sighs with me. From the look of his hollow cheeks, I'd say he doesn't get much to eat.

I tear a chunk from the sandwich and hold it out to him. His mouth falls open in amazement, like no one's ever shared food with him before.

"Go on." I thrust the piece at him.

Snatching it, he jams it in his mouth as if he's afraid I'll take back the offer. His cheeks bulge like a chipmunk, and as he chews, his eyelids flutter with delight.

We lick our fingers clean.

Mister Baker halts the carriage in front of a majestic entrance built in a white wall. "There it is! The new Saratoga Race Course," he announces with pride. "I'll give you a quick tour before we head to the stable."

We go through the gate. The grandstand is down the lane quite a distance. The rear of the building faces us, but it's so long I can't see either end from where I stand. A row of arched entryways stretches across the back like the pattern on the hem of a skirt.

A grove of pines shades both sides of the drive. "These are the cooling grounds," Mister Baker explains. "For between heats. The open area around the grandstand is for carriages. Ladies can step right from their carriages and walk into the grandstand."

He halts the buggy at the far-left end of the enormous grandstand. I have to tilt my head back to see the edge of the roof.

"The new grandstand can seat two thousand spectators," Mister Baker tells us. "Fifty cents to get in the gates. One dollar for the grandstand. Ladies can also watch from their carriages, and sporting men can watch from the lawn in front of the stand."

Through one of the entryways, I see a broad stairway sweeping to the seating area above. Itching to see where the stairs lead, I head toward them. But when Mister Baker says, "No colored patrons allowed," I quickly turn back. Seems the North has as many rules about coloreds as the south.

Short Bit holds the carriage horses while the two men climb from the buggy. I follow them, still leading Aristo, down a gravel walkway past the grandstand to a long white railing.

Leaning on the rail, I stare at the racetrack, open-mouthed. The dirt track is so wide, I can barely see across the infield to the backstretch. And it's so long, I can barely see the homestretch turn. The inside and outside rails are newly painted white and lush grass waves in the infield. I crane my neck to peer down the front stretch. There are two judges' towers, one on either side of the finish line. Casting a shadow over everything is the immense grandstand.

The sound of thundering hooves makes me glance across the infield. Two jockeys are galloping their mounts down the backstretch. They look like specks in the distance, but I can tell that one rider's white, one's black.

That might be Gilpatrick and Abe Hawkins! I think. Despite the heat, goose bumps rise on my arms. Suddenly, I understand Mister Giles's zeal to be here.

Taking the slack out of the rope, I draw Aristo close and cup my hands around his muzzle. "Aristo," I whisper. "In three days, that will be me and you. We're going to be galloping down that stretch, racing against some of the most famous horses and riders in the whole world. And colt, you better believe *we're gonna win!*"

CHAPTER ELEVEN

Gabriel, come over here." Mister Giles's summons breaks into my dream. "Mister Baker is telling me about the track."

"The Association graded the track so it's as level as a billiard table," Mister Baker's saying, "and measured it carefully so it's exactly a mile around. The surface is a mixture of sand and loam spread over two inches of clay, good footing for the horses. The turns are banked for safety."

Mister Giles claps Mister Baker on the back. "Why, you Saratogians think of everything."

"We aim to have the best racecourse in the country."

"Now we better get Aristo settled," Mister Giles says as we walk back to the carriage. "He's had a long journey. I'm eager to see your facilities, Mister Baker. Aristo is used to the finest care."

Mister Baker harrumphs. "Mister Giles, you must realize that I have a good number of charges to care for at the stable. Your colt will be one of many."

"I understand your concerns, Mister Baker. But I am paying for the best."

"And I will offer the best I can manage, considering the circumstances."

"Are you saying my money isn't good enough?"

"I'm saying your *horse* isn't good enough. Newspaper reporters and ticket buyers are flocking to the track to see the famous Kentucky and Tipperary, not your unraced colt."

"I realize the entries for this meet are top quality," Mister Giles replies somewhat haughtily. "That is why I entered Aristo, who is quite comparable, I can assure you!"

"Mister Giles, your colt will be racing in the Saratoga Chase against the unbeaten filly Lizzie H. and Cornelius Jeremiah's colt Faraway, who just won in St. Louis. No disrespect to you, sir, but the odds are low that your untried colt, ridden by an inexperienced colored boy, will have a chance. Your horse will be treated accordingly."

Mister Giles raises his chin. "I see." Stiffly, he climbs into the carriage.

As I follow the carriage down the lane, I pat Aristo's neck. "Don't listen to Mister Baker, 'Risto. *You're* the fastest colt, and soon all of Saratoga will know it."

The two men drive in silence to the Trotting Course, a large area dotted with barns, stables, and storage sheds.

Mister Baker shows us the stall. "Short Bit is at your service," he says. "Now unless you have any questions, I have some pressing matters to attend to."

"Thank you for your help." Mister Giles gives him a curt nod and then leads Aristo into the stall, while Short Bit and I unload the supplies. The instant we lift out the last sack, Mister Baker cracks the whip over the carriage horses and drives off.

"I suppose my name needs to be John Clay or Bob Lincoln to get fine treatment in Saratoga," Mister Giles muses to himself.

"You could have told Mister Baker that Aristo ran a 1:40 mile when he raced Nantura," I say.

He shoots me a frown. "That's between you and me, Gabriel," he says in a low voice. "Perhaps it's just as well the colt's considered a long shot." He grins suddenly. "That could be in our favor to win us some big money."

By the time Aristo's walked, brushed, and fed, it's late afternoon and my feet are dragging. Aristo's stall is at the end of the shed row away from the other horses. It's roomy, airy, and shaded by a few pine trees. The hay and straw are stored in a big barn nearby, and an empty stall serves as our supply and tack room. There's no turn-out paddock, but there is a field nearby where I can walk the colt and let him graze.

While Short Bit and I work, Mister Giles spends his time moseying around the Trotting Course, introducing himself to owners and trainers. When he's satisfied that Aristo is settled, he hires a carriage.

"I'll be back in the morning." He nods toward the other end of the barn. "Lizzie H. is stabled yonder. Her owner, Mister Sturgess, is mighty boastful. And I inspected

Faraway. The colt's nice enough, but Cornelius Jeremiah has more money than horse sense."

He winks and flips me several coins. "Get some rest and some vittles. I'll see you before the sun comes up. That's when we'll work Aristo. No need to show him off to all of Saratoga," he adds before leaving for town and his fancy room at the Congress Hotel.

I bid him good day, then look down at Short Bit. My stomach's rumbling like the train. "You think you could buy us *two* of those oyster sandwiches? One for me and one for you?"

His eyes light and he nods excitedly. I place the coins in his grimy palm and he races off. Pulling a barrel up to Aristo's stall, I sit on the wooden lid. The grounds are bustling with workers finishing up for the night. Some are sitting around, chewing tobacco and jawing. Hooks and Cuffy are shooting craps outside a stall. I've kept my eyes open for Jackson since we arrived, but I haven't spotted him yet. Sure would be nice to see a friendly face.

Aloneness settles over me. I wonder if Ma's settled in at Camp Nelson…if Pa's getting his cavalry organized…if Jase and Tandy are caring for Captain…and if Annabelle's teaching the field hands.

I miss them all with a powerful ache.

Behind me, I hear Aristo crunching hay. He sticks his head over the half door and bits of straw rain onto my shoulders. I reach up and tickle his whiskery muzzle. "I guess I ain't completely alone, huh, colt?"

Aristo lips my hair, all friendly like, and then goes back

to eating. He's happy and that's what matters, I decide with a huge yawn. That and proving to Mister Baker and all those other Northerners that a colored boy and a colt from Kentucky can win.

Resting my back against the door, the long day washes over me and I let my eyelids droop. I must have fallen asleep, because I'm startled awake by a tap on my shoulder. Short Bit's grinning at me. He's holding two brown wrapped sandwiches. I grin back, happy to see a friendly face. He plops one in my lap, then turns over a wooden bucket and sits next to me. We eat without talking, our slurps and belches the only sounds.

"Ahhh." Leaning back again, I pat my satisfied stomach. It's dusk, the air is cool, and the grounds are hushed. I'm feeling mighty drowsy when two boys saunter up and stop directly in front of us. One's white with scruffy sideburns; the other's colored with a half-bald head. They stand with their arms crossed against their chests and their legs akimbo like they've got a beef to pick. Beside me, Short Bit stiffens, instantly wary, as if he's had a run-in with them before. My scalp prickles.

The white boy addresses Short Bit. "Hey lack-brain. Why you sittin' with that Kentucky boy?"

"Maybe he's sitting there 'cause a *slave* and a halfwit are about equal," the colored boy says. "Don't ya think, Gordon?"

I avert my eyes and hold my tongue. Ain't no use telling them I ain't a slave. If they're aiming to pick a fight, it might make things worse.

Gordon directs his ire at Short Bit. "Where's that money

you owe us, halfwit?" he snaps. Short Bit gives a tiny shrug, and then, shifty as a fox, tries to dart off the bucket and run for it. But Gordon's expecting him to run. He snatches him by the collar and slams him against the wall. My heart's thumping so hard it hurts my ribs.

"And don't tell us you ain't got any money." Gordon nods at me. "We saw that darky paying you off. Bet he's bribing you to sneak into Faraway's stall tonight and poison his water, ain't he?"

Keeping my gaze on my lap, I say, "The money was for food."

The colored boy kicks the barrel I'm sitting on. "Shut up. We wasn't talkin' to you. We was talkin' to the halfwit. Short Bit owes us a quarter and we aim to get it."

My fingers tighten into fists. My anger's starting to churn up the oysters. "Quit calling him a halfwit."

Gordon snorts. "Why? He *is* a halfwit. Why else would they call him *Short* Bit? 'Cause the boy ain't a whole bit. He's missing two and a half cents. Two and a half *sense,* git it?"

I get it. Only I don't like it. The problem is, if I fight them, they'll beat me so badly I won't be able to ride. If I don't fight them, they're going to pummel Short Bit. Least now I know where he got his bruises.

I glance over at Short Bit, who's slouched on the bucket, head hanging like he's been beaten so many times that one more won't matter.

Only it *does* matter. I left the South hoping to see freedom. Only thing I found out so far is that skin color ain't the only reason folks beat you down.

Slowly, I stand and raise my eyes to them. Their faces are pocked and greasy; their clothes are as raggedy as Short Bit's.

"He'll give you the money tomorrow," I say, my words steady.

"Why should we believe *you?*" the colored boy sneers. "A slave who ain't got nothin'."

"We shouldn't believe him." Gordon grabs Short Bit by the collar and hauls him to his feet. "Quit talking, Danny. Let's punch the little weasel's teeth out, and next time he'll cough up that money right quick."

Gordon draws back his fist. Short Bit scrunches his eyes and turns his cheek. His arms hang limp like he's given up.

I shrug. "Go ahead. Hit him. Except all you'll have then are bloody knuckles. But if you wait until tomorrow, he'll pay you *fifty* cents."

Danny and Gordon look at each other with vacant expressions, like the offer is too tricky to calculate. "Where's he goin' to get fifty cents?" Danny asks.

"Same place he got money for sandwiches."

Gordon frowns as if thinking on it, then abruptly releases his grip. Short Bit drops like an empty sack. "Noon," he snaps. "And if he don't have fifty cents, you'll *both* git it. *Git* it?"

They saunter off, arms slung around each other's shoulders, laughing at their cleverness. When I glance down at Short Bit, he has tears in his eyes. He rubs them, leaving dirty streaks. Then, without a word, he jumps to his feet and races out of sight.

I sigh. Not that I expected thanks. An explanation, maybe, but not thanks.

I move the barrel away from the door, pick up a brush, and go inside Aristo's stall. The colt's eating the last of his hay. Earlier, he polished off half a bucket of grain, so I know he made the journey just fine.

Wish I could say the same for me. Except for Short Bit, Northerners seem mighty mean-spirited so far. As I brush Aristo, I recall Gordon's words: *Bet he's bribing you to sneak into Faraway's stall and poison his water.* It also seems that Northerners are as low-down as Southerners when it comes to winning races.

The idea sends a shiver up my spine. I vow not to leave Aristo's side.

★★★

The next morning I wake before dawn. Mister Giles wants to work Aristo early, so I need to check the colt's water and give him a flake of hay.

Draping the blanket around my shoulders, I open the stall door. Short Bit's outside, crouched on the ground, his arms hugging his bare legs. He springs up, a frightened glint in his eye, like he's ready for a cuff or a curse.

"I'm glad to see Gordon and Danny didn't beat you up last night," I say, hoping to ease his fear. Aristo sticks his head over the stall door and snuffles the boy's cheek. Eyes still on me, Short Bit reaches up to stroke the colt's neck. His clothes are filthy and he reeks of manure.

"Though you ain't none too clean," I add. "I'm surprised Aristo didn't spook when he took a whiff of you." Unwrapping the blanket, I fold it over my arm. "Well, I best get the colt fed and groomed. Could use some help. As I recall, someone needs to earn fifty cents to pay off those no-accounts."

Short Bit nods.

"Then let's get going."

With Short Bit's help, I get Aristo ready in time for Mister Giles, who shows up just as the sky's changing from black to gray. He's bright eyed and bearing biscuits with honey.

"Good morning!" he greets us as he opens the stall door and strides in. "I trust everyone slept well." He hands us each a gooey biscuit. I take a bite and close my eyes in rapture, deciding it tastes almost as heavenly as Cook Nancy's.

Mister Giles walks around Aristo, inspecting him. "Horse looks like a champion, Gabriel."

I jab a sticky thumb at Short Bit. "Aristo's groom helped, too, Mister Giles. And...um...he's usually tipped fifty cents. If that's all right with you, sir."

Mister Giles eyes Short Bit, who's stuffing a biscuit in his mouth with dirty fingers. I can't blame the man for his doubtful expression. If I saw the boy through his gentleman's eyes, I'd have to grimace, too.

Reaching in his pocket, Mister Giles hands Short Bit a half dollar. "If Gabriel has appointed you Aristo's official groom, then you must be worthy."

I lead the colt from the stall. The morning's gray and misty, and a few grooms are beginning to stir. Short Bit latches the rope to the snaffle ring, and Mister Giles gives me a leg up. Then he strides to a one-horse carriage tethered to a hitching post.

"Gabriel," he says, his eyes twinkling as he climbs into the buggy. "Last night, I met William R. Travers, president of the Saratoga Association. Quite a witty fellow. Tomorrow's Travers Stakes is named after him, you know."

I nod a scant reply, my attention on Aristo. He's so jubilant to be out of the stall that he's springing in the air. Short Bit grips the rope with both hands, determined to keep hold.

"All night I played the charming Southern gentleman," Mister Giles goes on, oblivious to the colt's antics. "When the evening ended, Mister Travers *personally* invited us to work Aristo on the Saratoga track."

"He did? Hurrah!" I whoop. Aristo leaps sideways, startling the carriage horse, which strains at its traces.

"Easy, easy!" Mister Giles hollers.

"Whoa. Whoa, now." I rein the colt in a tight circle. Short Bit stumbles after us. Mister Giles settles the buggy horse, and we head off briskly to the new track.

The grandstand's shrouded in fog, and the place is eerily quiet. Awe fills me. This will be Aristo's first gallop on a real track. Ever since I laid eyes on the colt, I knew he was special. Now I realize that Saratoga ain't just about my dreams. It's Aristo's chance, too.

Mister Giles drives the buggy around the grandstand and

parks by the gap in the railing. "Start off slow, Gabriel. The colt had a long journey. After he's warmed up—"

"Sir," I interrupt. "No disrespect, but the colt will tell me when he's ready."

"Right, right. Of course. Use your judgment."

Short Bit unhooks the rope, and I steer Aristo through the gap and onto the dirt track. The colt breaks into a trot, I rise in the saddle, and the worries of the past days and nights disappear in the rhythm of his stride.

Jogging past the grandstand, we round the turn to the backstretch. Aristo weaves wildly from side to side, jolting me with each bouncy step. He shakes his head, wanting to run, and I hum to him.

We trot once around the track. My cheeks grow damp from the mist; my fingers are slick on the reins. When Aristo again trots down the backstretch and his stride lengthens, I cluck. He breaks into a rocking canter, his muscles rolling like well-oiled wheels. His mouth feels soft in my hands, and steam rises from his sweaty neck.

He's ready.

I press my heels into his sides. That's all the colt needs. He flattens his ears, stretches out his long legs, and digs his hooves deep into the track's smooth surface.

As Aristo gallops around the homestretch turn, the morning air brushes my skin and a grin spreads across my face.

I'm on the greatest horse, at the greatest track—and it's the greatest feeling ever!

CHAPTER TWELVE

Aristo thunders down the homestretch. I keep a tight rein, holding him back, and the colt fights me the whole way. When we fly past the gap, Short Bit halloos from his perch on the railing. Mister Giles cheers from his seat in the buggy.

Through the mist I see the judges' towers, their peaked roofs rising above the fog. Aristo races past the finish line, and I raise my arm in pretend celebration.

A movement by the railing catches my eye. I glimpse the dark outline of a top hat, but we sail swiftly past, and I lose sight of whoever it is in the haze.

"Whoa, colt." Aristo roots his head, wanting to keep running. By the time I pull him to a trot and get him turned, the specter by the railing is gone. Were my eyes tricking me or had someone really been there?

As I trot past again, I spy a hunched form scuttling toward the grandstand, disappearing, ghostlike, into the fog. A chill tingles up my arms.

Someone *had* been there. And whoever it was had been watching Aristo and me.

"He looked terrific!" Mister Giles says as he and Short Bit run onto the track to meet us. Sitting deep in the saddle, I slow Aristo to a walk. I pat his neck, my chest bursting with pride, forgetting about the apparition.

Short Bit hooks the rope to Aristo's snaffle ring.

"I never let him run full out and he was still flying," I boast as I dismount. "If he can keep up that speed for a mile and three-quarters, we're going to leave those other horses in the dust!"

"I believe you're right," Mister Giles agrees excitedly. "The fog was too thick for me to get a perfect time, but I ticked it off in my head. He ran about a twenty-three-second quarter mile."

My jaw drops. I don't know how to count past my fingers, but I know enough to realize that Aristo's time is *fast*.

"And I believe we'll keep that information to ourselves." He levels a firm look at me, then at Short Bit. "No need for the competition to get wind of this colt's abilities."

"I'm afraid it may be too late for that, sir." I point toward the grandstand. "Someone was standing by the finish line when we galloped past. He might have had a watch, too, although I doubt he got a good time on account of the fog."

Mister Giles slaps his thigh. "I was afraid of that. Any idea who it was?"

"A man in a top hat."

Mister Giles sighs. "That description fits just about every sportsman, gambler, politician, and swindler in Saratoga.

Someone must have discovered we were going out early this morning."

Reaching up, he runs his hand down Aristo's neck, then turns back to me. I see the concern in his eyes. "The meet begins tomorrow. Aristo runs the next day. There will be folks who don't want this colt to win. We need to be extremely vigilant if Aristo's to have a fair chance."

"Yes sir." I peer over at Short Bit. He's gnawing his lip and his eyes won't meet mine.

That's when a horrible thought hits me. Short Bit owes no allegiance to Mister Giles, Aristo, or me. What if someone's paying him to report everything we do? How else did the man in the top hat find out we'd be on the track this early?

I narrow my eyes. I know all about spies. Both the Northern and Southern armies have spies in this war. And now that I think on it, it seems mighty odd that Short Bit's been dogging my heels ever since we arrived.

Might be *he's* a spy for someone who doesn't want Aristo to win. That means that outside of Mister Giles, there ain't no one I can trust at this track.

★★★

"Go, Abe, go!" I chant as the horses thunder down the homestretch. It's the first day of the Saratoga Meet and the end of the Travers Stakes, the most exciting race I've ever watched. Gilpatrick's in the lead riding Kentucky, Abe Hawkins on Tipperary is a nose behind, and the Morris colt runs third. Patti, ridden by the young jockey Billy Burgoyne, trails by two lengths; Ringmaster lags far behind, pretty much done for.

My eyes are on Abe. I'm leaning over the rail, men and boys pushing and shoving around me, watching his every move. He's hunched on Tipperary's neck, trying with all his skill to catch Kentucky. But his colt ain't going to do it. Neither whip nor spur will make a difference. I can tell by Tipperary's flat ears and high tail that he's played out, and Kentucky crosses the finish line ahead by several lengths.

I frown, pondering why Abe didn't win. The man rides even better than I expected. And Tipperary jumped to the lead. So what happened? Why'd the horse tucker out? What do I need to do tomorrow to make sure Aristo doesn't get skunked, too?

I vault over the railing, joining the boisterous crowd streaming onto the track. Dodging through the revelers, I make my way toward the judges' tower. Reporters, politicians, and track officials surround Gilpatrick and Kentucky. Mister John Hunter, Kentucky's owner, is holding up a shiny trophy. He's standing in the tower, giving a speech to all who will listen, which I gather is few. It is hard to make out his words over the deafening noise of the celebration.

I aim my sights again on Abe and Tipperary, standing off to one side. The jockey has just dismounted, and I hear Mister Ward, Tipperary's owner, boasting loudly to a few reporters. "We'll face Kentucky in Friday's Sequel Stakes and win. You have my promise on that!"

Abe stands quietly behind Mister Ward. Sweat trickles

down his solemn face, and now the reporters are calling out questions to *him*.

"Abe, Southerners rate you the best jockey in the world!" one shouts. "You think you'll keep that title in the North?"

"Tipperary was the favorite to win the Travers, Abe," another says. "You had such great success in St. Louis. What went wrong today?"

I turn my eyes to Abe, wanting to know the answers myself. But someone jostles me on his way past, and I miss the jockey's words completely.

Frustrated, I throw down my cap and stomp on it. Suddenly I see Abe parting the crowd, heading in my direction. I stare at him, speechless, until he's right on top of me. "Mister Hawkins," I blurt out, "I aim to be a famous jockey like you."

Smiling, he sets a hand on my head. "Then, son, b-b-be honest with your horse, and it'll give you its b-b-best," he says in his well-known stutter.

"Thank you," I whisper as he passes on by, a swarm of folks clamoring after him. I can still feel the pressure of his hand, and I think on his words: *Be honest to your horse and it'll give you its best.*

Sounds like Pa's advice, and I'm going to follow it.

I'm pushing my way toward the railing when someone shoves me hard in the back. I pitch forward onto the track. Folks stride right on by me without stopping to help. Then I feel the nudge of a boot in my side. Flipping over, I look up. Danny and Gordon are staring down at me, amusement in their eyes. Short Bit hovers like a shadow behind them.

"Hey, Kentucky boy, you owe us fifty cents."

I bridle. "Short Bit paid you. Why should I give you money?"

"You want your horse to stay safe?" Danny kicks me in the ribs.

Pain shoots up my side, making my eyes water. But the thought of them even touching Aristo makes me sick. "Yes," I reply through clenched teeth.

"Then you'll pay us." Danny brings back his foot for another kick, but the stewards hustle over. "Move on, boys!" they order. "Move on and clear the track for the next race."

I jump to my feet. Gordon and Danny flash me nasty grins and join the throng leaving the track. For an instant, Short Bit stares at me, his eyes wild, a fresh bruise blackening one cheek. Then he whirls around and disappears after them.

Bile rises in my throat. I'm growing weary of greedy, mean-spirited folks. Then a stab of worry replaces the pain in my ribs.

Aristo. This morning, Mister Giles paid a guard to keep an eye on the colt while we watched the Travers. After Danny's threat, do I dare trust *anyone?*

Breaking into a run, I weave around the spectators and revelers, dash from the track, and run down the lane. By the time I reach the Trotting Course and Aristo's barn, my insides are bursting.

The guard's asleep outside Aristo's stall. The colt thrusts his head over the half door, and greets me with a lusty whinny.

116

Doubling over, sides heaving, I groan with relief.

Fingers circle my upper arms and I'm jerked upright. Gordon and Danny flank me. Danny sticks his face in mine. "Got that money?"

I shake my head. Their fingers tighten around my arms, burning my skin.

"We want it *now.*" Gordon says.

"I ain't got any money," I choke out, still breathless. "And even if I did, I wouldn't give it to you!" I add, struggling to break their hold on me. Pa always told me to think long and hard before laying a hand on a critter or another person. But I've had enough and I'm ready to fight.

"You wanna bet?" Danny growls.

I narrow my eyes. "Go ahead. I've been beaten and whipped by fellows meaner and sorrier than you two." I glare at them with false bravado. My heart's hammering beneath my ribs, but my gaze bores into theirs until Danny glances uneasily away.

"Don't pay those threats no mind," Gordon tells Danny, but there's no fire in his words now. "Pat him down. See if he has any money."

Danny lets go of me and steps back. "You pat him down."

"No, *you* do it," Gordon snaps. "I've got hold of him!"

Seeing my chance, I yank my arm from Gordon's grasp and whirl to face them. "Ain't *neither* of you going to pat me down." Raising my fists, I stand my ground.

Aristo bangs the door with his hoof, and the guard wakes with a start.

"Ho, you boys get outta here," he shouts, and, turning tail, Gordon and Danny run off. I lower my fists. *Thank you, Jesus,* I murmur, my moment of courage spent.

I wish I could believe that I've seen the end of those two.

★★★

Someone's shaking my shoulder. Hard. Fingers dig into my flesh. I jerk awake. It's night, and I'm curled in the corner of Aristo's stall. It's so dark that at first I can't see. Then two eyes blink at me.

"Git out," a voice hisses. "Git Aristo out. *Now!*" The last word is an urgent plea. I push myself to my feet just in time to see Short Bit steal from the stall, leaving the door ajar.

I smell something burning.

I rush to Aristo, who's frozen in place, his nostrils quivering. Sticking my head over the half door, I see smoke billowing from a stall farther down the shed row.

The barn's on fire!

Reaching around the doorway, I whip the rope off the hook and snap it to Aristo's halter. I open the door, trying to keep my movements calm. The smoke's so thick, I can barely see the other end of the barn. I hear the crackle of burning wood and the squeal of a terrified horse.

Aristo's trembling. "Come on, colt," I croon. "Don't get ornery on me. We've got to get out of here."

I twine my fingers through his mane, chirp encouragingly, and lead him in the opposite direction from the fire. The colt breaks into a nervous jog, and we hurry into the night air. When we're out of danger, I turn. The fire's moving slowly, fanning out toward both ends of the barn.

Is this Gordon and Danny's handiwork?

In the glow of the flames, I see several workers forming a bucket brigade. Fire is a stable's worst nightmare—hay and straw are ready fuel for flames—and a bucket brigade will be scant help. It won't take long before the fire reaches Aristo's stall.

I hear the horse squeal again. *Lizzie H.* The mare was the only horse stabled at the other end. Is someone going after her? Or is it too late?

"I've got to help her, 'Risto." Quickly, I lead him to a small barn far from the fire. There's an empty stall, rarely used, judging by the moldy smell. I guide Aristo inside, step out of the stall, and latch the door securely behind me. I know I shouldn't leave him. But I couldn't live with myself if I stood by and watched a horse burn to death.

Rope in hand, I race toward the far end of the blazing barn. I crane my neck, trying to see Lizzie. Flames haven't reached her stall, but the smoke's thick, and the bottom door's shut. Did someone get her out already?

Then I see her muzzle poke over the half door. Her eyes are white with fear and she's screaming as if in agony. Holding my breath, I plunge toward her through the smoke. When I open the door, she throws herself backward. Ain't no way I can catch her. She's too scared. I fling the door wide and stand back.

"Run, Lizzie, giddup! Get out of there!" I wave my arms in the air, shooing her. She just stands there, trembling. I've heard of horses growing crazy from the fear and the smoke. It looks like Lizzie's lost her wits, all right.

I step inside. "Come on, pretty mare," I croon. "You've got to get out of here. *Fast.*"

She rears high, her forelegs pawing the smoke-filled air. Frantic, she lunges toward the open door, and I dive out of the way. My head hits her feed bucket, and for a second I'm dazed.

Then smoke covers me like a thick blanket.

Holding my breath, I fight my way to my feet. I can't see a thing! Panic fills me. I blink and stretch out my hand, feeling for the door. Turning right, I slam into the wall. My eyes sting. Closing them against the burning, I grope along the wall. I gasp, unable to hold my breath any longer. My lungs fill with the acrid air, and I double over, coughing and retching.

I turn left and move slowly, using the wall as a guide, but I crash into the feed bucket again and fall to my knees. My innards feel seared, my eyes are blind, and I can only hope for a quick end.

CHAPTER THIRTEEN

Strong hands cup my armpits and drag me through the straw and out the door. When I hit the cool air, I cough so long and hard I fear my ribs will crack. Then someone hands me a cup of water and I drink.

"Gabriel, use this water to wash out your eyes and nose."

Gabriel. The person knows who I am. I peer through slitted eyes. *It's my old friend Jackson!*

He's crouched beside a bucket, holding a dipper of water.

"J-Jackson!" I stammer, and then I'm overcome with another coughing fit.

He slaps me on the back. "Hack it out, boy." Using a rag, he splashes water over my head and neck until I'm drenched and cool.

"Is Lizzie H. all right?" I finally speak, my voice scratchy.

"She's fine, thanks to you."

"And Aristo?"

"I posted a groom by his door for safekeeping."

Fear must have lit my face, because he adds quickly,

"Don't worry. It's a boy I trust." He frowns and his gaze goes back to the burning barn. "Not many you can trust round here."

My shoulders slump wearily. All my vigilance almost didn't pay off. All my false bravado didn't help matters, either. *Aristo. Lizzie H.* Both horses could have been killed in the fire. *And me, too,* I think with a shudder.

"You saying someone set the barn on fire?" I whisper hoarsely.

"I ain't sayin' it aloud. Too many ears."

I swallow, my throat dry and hot. I picture Short Bit stealing from Aristo's stall. Did Gordon and Danny set the fire? Did Short Bit help them? If so, why did he warn me to get out?

I study the men passing buckets down the line and throwing water on the fire, which, thankfully, is almost out. Danny and Gordon and Hooks and Cuffy are among them; there's no sign of Short Bit.

Bending over the bucket, I splash my face. Then I wipe it with the rag. The men are standing back now, staring at the soggy, charred walls and blackened roof of the barn.

I rise to my feet. "Looks like the danger's over," I say to Jackson. "I best see to Aristo. Why don't you come with me? See if the colt remembers your ugly face."

"Ugly to *you*, maybe, but handsome to the ladies," he jokes.

I laugh. "It's sure good to see you, Jackson. Thanks for pulling me out of the fire."

"It's not exactly what I had planned for this evening,"

Jackson says as we set off across the grounds. He's dressed all stylish in a vest, silk shirt, and checked britches. A matching checked cap tilts rakishly on his slicked-back hair.

Jackson chortles. "Dang, boy, I couldn't believe my eyes when I saw you lead Aristo into that empty stall and then run to help Lizzie. "What's *Gabriel Alexander* doing in Saratoga?" I asked myself. Then I remembered Mister Giles talking a while back about bringing a horse to the meet, and it all made sense." He shakes his head. "Only a fool Kentucky boy would rescue a horse from a burning stall."

"You were once a fool Kentucky boy. Must be why you rescued me."

"You callin' me a fool?" Jackson raises his fists. For a second we spar, punching air. Then, grinning at each other, we fall into step again.

"How long you been in Saratoga?" I ask. "I looked for you when we first arrived."

"Been here in New York State since I left Woodville. I'm jockeying for Doctor Crown, who has a farm south of here. I work his horses at the Saratoga track a lot. This afternoon we brought two horses for the meet."

"You a famous jockey yet?" I tease.

"I'm gettin' there."

"What races are you riding in? Not the Saratoga Chase, I hope."

"Naw. I'm jockeying a mare named Diamond Girl in the Saratoga Stakes. And a colt named Charley Riley in a hurdle race."

"A hurdle race? What's that?"

"A race over jumps."

I stop in my tracks. "No. You're joshing me, Jackson."

"I ain't. I learned how to jump a horse since I've been in New York. Learned lots of things since I been in New York." He winks roguishly, and I gather the things he's learned would make Ma blush.

"So you like it here in the North?"

"I do. It takes getting used to. But all in all, I've found being here right powerful. Not so many folks giving you suspicious glances and asking for free papers."

"I wish I could say the same about being in the North." I slow as I approach Aristo's stall. Sitting on the ground, back against the door, is a light-skinned Negro. When he sees Jackson, he jumps to his feet. "Kept my eye on him, just like you wanted, Mister Jackson. No one bothered him, but the colt seems spooked."

"Thanks, Riff. Now go back and tell Angel to fix up that spare stall for this horse." Jackson gives Riff a coin, and the boy hurries off. "That's one of Doctor Crown's grooms. He's a good worker." His eyes twinkle. "And his sister's real pert, too."

"Why, Jackson, you ain't changed a bit." Laughing, I open the stall door. "It's all right, 'Risto," I soothe. The colt's stomping and twitching, and he pushes me with his nose like he's mad I ain't been around.

"Are you saying I can keep 'Risto over where Doctor Crown's stabling his horses?" I ask Jackson.

"I'm saying it. You can't put the colt in that burned-out

barn. Doctor Crown's a fair man and he'll understand the situation. Tomorrow morning, Mister Giles can make whatever arrangements he wants."

"Thanks. It'll be good to have the colt someplace safe." As we walk Aristo to the other barn, I tell Jackson about my run-in with Hooks and Cuffy on the train and my suspicions about Gordon, Danny, and Short Bit.

"I don't know those first fellows you're naming," Jackson replies, "but that Danny and Gordon ain't worth spit. I doubt those two boys have a smart thought between them. If they did start the fire, someone put them up to it."

"What about Short Bit?"

"Naw. Short Bit didn't start the fire. He loves horses. He ain't got no ma or pa, so horses are like his family."

I'm glad to hear Jackson's opinion of Short Bit, but it don't mean I wholly trust the boy. "He ain't got no ma or pa?" I repeat, the thought amazing me.

"That's what's known as an orphan," Jackson explains.

"You're getting pretty smart, Mister Jackson," I jest.

"You best believe it. This way." He gestures toward a small barn nestled in a grove of pines.

"I did note that 'Risto took an instant liking to Short Bit."

"All the horses like Short Bit. That's 'cause he's more horse than person. Mister Baker lets him live in the barns, but I swear he treats the boy worse than a slave."

"Why does Short Bit hang around with Danny and Gordon?"

"He don't. Danny and Gordon seek him out. Saratoga is all about entertainment. And bullying Short Bit's their entertainment."

I think about Short Bit's new bruise. "Ain't entertaining to him. Or me."

"Well, don't be sticking up for Short Bit, or Danny and Gordon will make you pay."

I don't tell Jackson they've already tried to make me pay.

We head into the second barn, lit by a kerosene lamp sitting against one wall. Stalls are built on both sides of a wide dirt aisle, reminding me of the barns back home. As we walk past, several horses greet Aristo with sleepy whickers.

"Over here, Jackson." A man holding a hay fork gestures from the open doorway of a stall. In the lamplight his skin glows a rich mahogany brown, and his long, pitch-black hair is plaited in two braids

I gape at the man. He's dressed in a work shirt and jeans, and he's barefoot like me. But he's not colored, nor is he white. He's like nothing I've ever seen.

"That's Angel," Jackson says in a low voice. "He's an Indian. He has a hard-to-say Indian name, so everyone just calls him Angel 'cause he can handle even a devil of a horse."

"An Indian?" I've never heard of such a person before.

"Mohawk. Best horseman I've ever met—other than your pa." When we near the stall, Jackson raises his voice. "Angel, meet Gabriel and Aristo," he says, as I lead the colt into the stall. "Gabriel, this is Angel."

"H-howdy do," I stammer before the Indian slips out of sight.

"A man of few words," Jackson says with a shrug.

The stall is bedded with clean straw and the rack filled with sweet hay. I unhook the rope, pat Aristo, and shut the door. Aristo turns several times, sniffs every corner, nickers to the other horses, and then begins eating.

Propping my arms on the closed door, I let out a weary sigh. Now that Aristo's safe, a weight lifts off my shoulders.

"How's your pa?" Jackson asks. He's standing beside me, a piece of straw clamped between his teeth.

"Pa's a corporal now," I tell him. "In charge of organizing a colored cavalry."

Jackson whistles. "Soon he'll be running Camp Nelson."

"And he helped Captain Waite rescue Mister Giles's horses from a band of raiders," I brag on.

Jackson tips back his cap. "Do tell!"

I launch into the tale, not forgetting to mention my own heroics. I push up my sleeve and show off my scar. "That's where a Rebel bullet creased my skin. But thanks to quick wits—and the cavalry—the raiders didn't get one horse. Mister Giles was so grateful that he gave me my freedom."

"Why, Gabriel, that's powerful good news! What else happened after I left?"

"Mistress Jane died a few weeks back and gave Annabelle her freedom, too. Ma's joined Pa at Camp Nelson. She's laundering clothes. And even though we saved Woodville from One Arm's raiders, those cowardly Rebels stole Captain from me and Jase one day when we were on our way home from Lexington." I tell him the story of meeting

Butler and Keats and how Newcastle cheated Mister Giles out of the reward money.

"You had *two* run-ins with guerrillas?" Jackson exclaims. "I'm amazed you ain't dead."

I shrug like it's no big thing. "Now that I look back on it, I'd rather face those Rebels any day than some of the Northerners I've met. At least I *know* the Rebels are snakes."

"I hope all that didn't make you forget your dream about being a famous jockey."

"Oh, I'm still dreamin'. I've won two races since you left." I nod toward Aristo. "And I'm aiming to win the Saratoga Chase on that colt, and get my name in the newspaper."

"Excuse me!" A voice breaks into our talk.

I spin around. A man's storming down the aisle between the stalls, waving a cane. He's wearing a formal evening suit and a stovepipe hat, and in the lamplight his face looks menacing. Beside him, a second man in dusty work clothes tries to keep up.

"Mister Sturgess, what brings you here this late hour?" Jackson asks, sounding surprised.

Raising his cane, Mister Sturgess whacks my shoulder. "This colored boy brings me here. My groom Langley," he points the tip of his cane at the man in work clothes, "says he saw this boy here *set the barn on fire!* I nearly lost one of my most valuable horses because of him."

I'm so startled by his words that I suck in a mouthful of air and start coughing again.

Jackson draws himself up. "Beg your pardon, Mister Sturgess. Gabriel here saved your mare. That's why he was in her stall. And he almost died getting her out."

"Doesn't make him innocent." Mister Sturgess raps me on the arm with the cane. "His master's horse is entered in tomorrow's race against Lizzie H. That's reason enough to accuse him—to accuse them *both* of setting that fire to keep my mare from beating their horse."

Jackson—a head shorter than this white man, and colored to boot—doesn't hesitate to defend me. "Sir, I know Gabriel and Mister Giles. Neither would do what you're accusing them of."

Mister Sturgess scowls at him. "Are you doubting Langley's word?"

"With all due respect, sir, why don't you smell Langley's breath? Then ask him why he was drinking whiskey with the other grooms instead of watching your horse."

Mister Sturgess tightens his jaw. His gaze shifts to Langley, who suddenly beats a hasty retreat from the barn.

"Perhaps I was too quick to judge," Mister Sturgess says, and strides off after Langley.

"Apology accepted," Jackson mutters.

I blow out my breath. "Whew. I was feeling the noose around my neck."

"They're not as quick to hang coloreds up here, Gabriel."

"Thanks for saving me, Jackson—that's twice now." I remember once calling Jackson a coward because he didn't want to enlist in the army with Pa. Now I know there are many kinds of bravery.

He shakes his head, grinning. "How's one boy get in so much trouble?"

I shake my head, too, not sure myself. "Earlier you said someone may have set the fire, and it looks like Mister Sturgess thought so, too. We know it wasn't me. And you say it wasn't Short Bit. Then who?"

Taking off his cap, Jackson runs his hand over his slicked-back hair. "I wish I knew. You know how it is on the track. Nobody trusts anyone. And for good reason. There are high stakes at this meet, and I don't mean just the purse money. Jockeys and owners want to strut down Broadway. They want to read their names in the paper. And they want their horses to head to the St. Louis meet as winners, not losers."

"That sounds like what you and me want."

"Only we want to earn it fairly." Jackson settles his cap back on his head. "Get some sleep. Angel will keep an eye on Aristo. You got a big day tomorrow."

"I'm still sleeping in the stall with the colt. But I would like to get my supplies first."

Jackson frowns. "You stay right here. Angel and I will fetch your supplies." He juts his chin toward the barn door. "Out there at night is nothing but trouble for a boy like you."

Trouble. A shiver travels up my spine. For certain, I don't need any more trouble.

CHAPTER FOURTEEN

Aristo nuzzles my shoulder, and my eyes shoot open. It's race day. I ain't but moments awake—and it's hours before the Saratoga Chase—but already my stomach's knotted with excitement.

This is it, I think. This is the day I've been waiting for.

I stretch my arms from the blanket and roll over—right on top of a straw-covered lump.

With a startled yelp, I spring back the same instant the lump shoots up from the straw. It's Short Bit. His blond hair's tangled, his lashes sprinkled with chaff.

"You scared me half to death!" I exclaim.

His eyes are as big as dinner plates, so I know he's just as surprised. Aristo sidles over, nudges me on the arm again, and sniffs Short Bit's head.

"Could have warned me you were goin' to sleep here." I wrap my blanket closer. Short Bit continues to stare at me, his shoulders rigid. The bruise on his eye matches his sooty cheeks, and his clothes smell like smoke.

I ain't seen the boy since he warned me about the fire.

My thoughts are still muddled. *Did* Short Bit have anything to do with the fire? And if not—as Jackson believes—then does he know who set it?

After a few minutes, I throw off my blanket. Immediately, the boy stiffens and that wary look creeps across his face again. "Don't worry," I say. "I ain't blaming you for the fire."

I get to my feet and stroke the colt's neck, my back to the boy. "But it might be that you saw who *did* set it. Might be that's why you're so afraid." I tilt my head so I can glimpse him over my shoulder.

Short Bit's folded into himself, arms tight against his stomach. He's rocking on his bottom, his eyes shut, and I gather my hunch is right. He does know something, and it's made him truly afraid.

My heart feels heavy. I've got a ma, a pa, a home, and in my whole life I've never been as fearful—or as alone—as Short Bit.

"Anyway, thanks for warning me. You saved my life, Short Bit."

He opens one eye.

I grin and whack Aristo on the neck. "More importantly, you saved this soon-to-be famous racehorse. And for that, I will be forever in your debt."

"Gabriel!" A voice bellows through the barn. "Rise and shine!"

I hurry over to the stall door. Jackson's striding down the aisle, dressed as natty as ever. "We're going out on the town," he declares.

I frown at him. "What are you talking about? It's race day. I ain't going to town."

"Yes sir, you are." He stops in front of the stall. "Angel and Riff will be here all morning to watch your horse. The Saratoga Chase ain't until afternoon. You can't spend your entire trip cooped up in that stall. So let's go. And bring that urchin, too." He jabs his thumbs toward Short Bit.

"I can't leave Aristo. It's too risky."

"You have no choice. Mister Giles has *ordered* you to leave. He's even lent us his buggy. He wants you, his jockey, rested for the big race—and he wants you clean."

"But I ain't dirty," I protest.

"Don't get all huffy with me, boy. This afternoon you and Short Bit will be parading Aristo past all the gentle-folk in the grandstand. Mister Giles doesn't want to hide his head with embarrassment 'cause you two look like beggars."

He runs his gaze down me. "That's all the clothes you've got?"

"Shirt and britches. What's wrong with that?"

"You look like a field hand. 'Bout time you dressed like a jockey."

I bristle. "A jockey doesn't need to look like a dandy to be a great rider."

"A jockey also doesn't need to look like he's been plowing the fields. Now quit arguing and let's go."

I poke my chin out, all stubborn-like.

Jackson sighs. "Gabriel, you can't defy Mister Giles's orders. Besides, don't you want to see Saratoga Lake?

Sample the milk punch and fried potatoes at Moon's Lake House?"

I prick up my ears. "Fried potatoes?"

"Called Saratoga Chips. Tastiest treat ever."

"And Mister Giles *ordered* me?"

"Afraid so."

"All right. I'll go. Only Angel and Riff have to promise they won't take their eyes off 'Risto. And we need to be back in plenty of time for the race."

"Promise."

I tell the horse goodbye, give Angel and Riff instructions, and leave with Jackson and Short Bit. I climb onto the carriage seat, and Short Bit kneels behind. Jackson unties the horse, and moments later we're clipping down East Congress Street into town. Even though it's early, tourists and race goers swarm the streets like ants.

Our first stop is a clothing shop tucked in an alley. Its tidy front room is filled with shelves and racks of clothes. A pretty colored lady who smells like Mistress Jane's roses waits on us. She sizes me and Short Bit up with a glance, then walks along the racks and shelves pulling off clothes, the whole while giggling with Jackson.

When we leave, our arms are piled high with packages. Our next stop is the bathhouse.

"Bring your new clothes in with you," Jackson says as he climbs from the carriage. Short Bit and me don't know what to make of a bathhouse, so neither of us moves. Jackson pulls us from the buggy by our ears.

A woman as round as a rain barrel meets us in the

doorway. She's wearing a damp apron and a colorful head-scarf. When she sees Short Bit, she frowns so crossly at him that he draws in his head like a turtle. "This bathhouse is for coloreds only," she tells Jackson.

Jackson snorts. "Sadie, this boy is so dirty he might as well be colored. 'Sides, he's an *orphan.*" He heaves a sad sigh. "Who else is going to wash him?"

Sadie's fierce eyes melt. "No mama? Oh my, oh my. Come here, young'un." Grabbing Short Bit, she pulls him against her plump belly. "We'll get you fixed up. Could be under all that dirt, you're a right handsome poppet."

Still pressing Short Bit to her skirt, Sadie leads us down a hall. "Room's all ready. When you need rinse water, just ring the bell."

She releases Short Bit and stands back. I step around her. The small room is even warmer and steamier than the summer day. There are two long tubs filled to the brim with water. Thick drying rags hang on pegs, and washrags, a bell, and two chunks of soap sit on a shelf between the tubs.

"Have at it, boys," Jackson says, adding in a serious tone, "and make sure you scrub with *soap* or Sadie'll come back and do it for you."

As Sadie and Jackson leave, she twitters and slaps his arm. "Oh, Mister Jackson, you are one to tease. Though I do enjoy scrubbing your back."

The door closes and Short Bit and me stare at each other. I ain't never undressed in front of anyone except Ma, and that was when I was little. And Short Bit looks like he ain't *never* taken off his filthy clothes.

I stick my finger in the water. I pick up the soap and smell it. Suddenly I hear a splash behind me, and water splats me on the back of the head.

I whirl. Short Bit's in the tub, water up to his chin. Grinning mischievously, he splashes me again.

I swipe the droplets from my eyes. Reaching into the tub, I flip water on him. It turns into a wild fight, and soon I'm drenched. Still wearing my clothes, I slide headfirst into the other tub.

We're enjoying ourselves, lolling in the soapy water, when Jackson sticks his head round the door. "Out, you two. My stomach's growling. That means it's time for Moon's Lake House. Sadie's bringing in two rinse buckets. Then dress and let's be on our way."

Two shakes later, we're driving past the Saratoga Race Course gate and on to the lake. I'm smelling so sweet and feeling so scratchy in my new clothes that I don't recognize myself. And there ain't nobody going to recognize Short Bit. He's scrubbed pink and wearing clean clothes that fit. Jackson even threw away Bit's porkpie hat and bought us gentlemen's sporting caps to match his own.

It's about a two-mile jaunt. When the buggy reaches a cleared area in the trees and I glimpse the lake, my mouth falls open. I've seen ponds and rivers but never a lake like this, which appears to stretch as wide and blue as the sky.

There's lots of buggy traffic, and dust is thick. Jackson pulls off to one side to point out sailboats, a steamboat, and smaller rowboats, all filled with gentlemen in bowlers and ladies holding parasols.

"How big is the lake?" I ask. "As big as an ocean?" I've heard about oceans from Annabelle, but I've never even seen a picture of one.

"Yonder is the far shore," Jackson replies, pointing across the lake to a mound of tree-covered land far in the distance. "If you have all day, you can ride around the lake."

Jackson grins at me and then looks over his shoulder at Short Bit. "Next stop's Moon's Lake House. Who's hungry?"

We both whoop. Moon's Lake House sits high on a hill that overlooks the lake. As Jackson drives the buggy around back, I glimpse ladies and gents strolling along walkways that lead to the lake. Other fine-looking folk are sitting on benches, sipping from stemmed glasses.

"Place will be packed, but George is expecting us." Jackson stops the buggy by a hitching rail near the kitchen entrance.

I jump from the seat. "George?"

"George Crum. He's the chef. He's the one who fries those tasty chips. I told him it's about time he quits working for Mister Moon and starts up his own eating-place. Short Bit, you stay with the horse and carriage. Gabriel will bring you a plate."

Short Bit nods agreeably, but I can't believe my ears. In Kentucky, colored folks never give orders to whites. Even the little white children boss around the slaves.

As Jackson and I walk away, I ask, "How come Short Bit can't come?"

"Cause he's a groom, Gabriel. You're a jockey. In the

137

North, there's a big difference. People treat jockeys with respect."

I frown as I puzzle over this respect thing. It's not unfamiliar to me. Mister Giles respected Pa. And Pa's soldiers respect him. But *white* people respecting *colored* jockeys? Must be why Jackson likes New York and why Abe Hawkins gets his name written up in the Northern newspapers.

I bob my head. "I like the sound of respect."

Jackson chuckles. "Course, folks love you when you're riding winners and have money in your wallet. Soon as you're riding losers and your wallet's empty, you eat in the buggy like Short Bit. Or you don't eat at all."

A colored lady meets us at the back door. Her glossy black hair is swept in a bun, and she's wearing a fashionable hoop skirt. "Well, Mister Jackson, it's about time you came back."

Jackson winks at her. "Couldn't keep me away, Miss Lacey." He introduces me and I whip off my cap. Taking my hand, the lady shakes it as if I'm a gentleman. "Pleased to meet you, Gabriel."

I blush. She's slightly older than Annabelle and almost as pretty.

"Your table is ready, sirs." She gracefully gestures to a round table and two chairs set up under a tree. Two colored men in day suits already occupy a second table, and a third is empty.

I twirl the cap in my hands, not sure what to do. I ain't never been in an eating establishment, nor had a pretty lady show me to my seat. I cut my eyes to Jackson, following his lead. He pulls out a chair, sits down, and places a linen napkin on his lap.

I slip into the chair opposite his, and tuck the napkin in my lap. Miss Lacey immediately brings us two drinks in frosty mugs made of *glass*. I take a sip of the concoction, glorying in the sweet taste. Then I lean over the table and whisper, "This must be milk punch."

"It is." Jackson raises his glass in a toast. His drink is a golden color and I can only guess what Miss Lacey spiked it with. "Here's to first place in our races," he says. "And to fame, to freedom, and to the North." I raise my glass, and we clink them together.

"Jackson, I still ain't figured out the North. If colored folks are free and colored jockeys respected," I ask between sips, "how come we can't eat inside with the whites?"

He sets down his glass. "Freedom don't mean the rules are the same for black and white, Gabriel. Maybe if the North wins this war, things will change."

This war. Abruptly, I lower my glass. In all the hustle and bustle and worries, I'd forgotten about the war!

Just then a tall man wearing a floppy white cap strides through the kitchen door. His dark face glistens with sweat, his apron is grease-stained, and he smells like Ma's lard-fried potatoes. A rolled-up newspaper is clutched in one hand, a heaping plate in the other.

"Jackson!" He waves the newspaper at us. "Miss Lacey said you were here. Glad you made it back."

"I wouldn't miss your potatoes for anything, George."

The man sets the plate between us. It's filled with small, golden-crisp slices of potato. Jackson quickly helps himself to a handful.

I snatch several chips, too, and pop them in my mouth. They're hot, crunchy, and salty, and I just about swoon. I'm reaching for another handful when George pulls up a chair and plops down. His face is grave. "Have you heard the news?"

"Which news?" Jackson asks. "That the fire at Mister Baker's barn might have been set on purpose? Or that the long shot colt Aristo's a sure bet to win in this afternoon's Saratoga Chase?" He winks at me.

"Forget the races. I'm talking about the war."

I stop chewing and listen closely. Maybe not everybody's forgotten about the war.

George unrolls the newspaper. "On July thirtieth, three hundred and thirty-five Union soldiers were killed by Rebels in Petersburg, Virginia," he reads. "One hundred and eight of them were black soldiers."

Shaking his head, he closes the paper. "Jackson, this war has gone on too long, and too many have died."

I try to swallow my mouthful of chips. It's hard to cipher three hundred, but even ten dead soldiers would be too many. The same day I was parading through Saratoga like a tourist, Rebel bullets were cutting down those Union soldiers.

A wave of sadness washes over me. I think of Ma scrubbing army uniforms and Pa drilling his men. I think of the runaway slaves enlisting at Camp Nelson, hoping for freedom, and I'm ashamed that I'm eating Moon's fried chips and worrying about a horse race when others are dying.

CHAPTER FIFTEEN

L ater, when we're driving back to the Trotting Course, I ask Jackson how we can think about winning a race when soldiers are dying in Petersburg.

Jackson gestures to the carriages passing by. "You think these rich white folks going to Moon's Lake care about the war?" He shakes his head. "Naw. They're drinking wine, planning what to wear to tonight's soiree, and making bets on the horses."

"Don't they know the war's important?" I persist. "That folks are fighting for freedom?"

He steers the buggy horse around an open-sided road coach filled with gaily dressed ladies and gentlemen. They eye us suspiciously, like we're vagabonds. "You know what I've discovered 'bout freedom since I've been in the North, Gabriel?" Jackson asks. "Freedom's about *money*. And to get that money, so you can really be free, you've got to work hard, and you've got to have a skill. And Gabriel, you and me have a skill: it's called jockeying a horse. If rich folks want to pay us for riding in races, then by golly, that's how we'll find freedom."

Slapping the reins sharply, he grunts in disdain. "Unless you want to die in the war. I gather that's one way coloreds can be free from the injustices on this earth."

"I don't want to die," I say quickly.

"I didn't think so." Jackson smiles. "You're more like me than you want to admit, Gabriel."

Falling silent, I ponder his words. Behind me, Short Bit's using his fingers to scoop fries and eggs into his mouth. The boy's white and free, yet he has no kind of life. I rub my forehead, itchy under my new cap. Even here in the North, the truth about freedom ain't so easy to grasp.

Soon the buggy turns into the Trotting Course, which bustles with grooms, owners, trainers, and horses. My pulse quickens, and I forget my pondering.

"How much time before the Saratoga Chase?" I ask Jackson.

"Plenty." He claps me on the back. "I'll be rootin' for you, Gabriel."

"Thanks. I'll be rootin' for you, too." I start to jump from the carriage when he stops me with a hand on my arm. I look over my shoulder at him. His face is grave. "Don't ever give up on those dreams of yours, Gabriel. Whatever you decide they are."

I nod, leap from the carriage, and run into the barn. Short Bit's on my heels, still shoveling fries in his mouth. Aristo stares white-eyed over the half-door like he's expecting us. Grinning, I cup his muzzle, but he tosses his head as if to say, "Let's get going!"

While Short Bit cleans the stall, I take Aristo for a long walk. Then we groom him until he shines like a new penny. The whole time, we're working quiet but together, like Pa and me used to do.

I'm brushing out Aristo's tail and Short Bit's picking out a front hoof when I catch him peering up at me. I give him a grin, and for the first time since our run-in with Danny and Gordon, he grins back. Somehow I know—just like I know a horse's heart—that Short Bit would never harm Aristo or any other horse. *Or me.*

"Short Bit!" someone hollers, and we both jump. For an instant, the boy cowers. Then he drops Aristo's hoof and darts from the stall, slamming the door behind him.

I look out. Mister Baker's standing in the doorway of the barn, the sunlight behind him. I can see the outline of his top hat and his hunched back.

My eyes widen as I suddenly recognize that odd shape. *Mister Baker* was the specter by the railing! But why was he watching Aristo? He has no entry in the Saratoga Chase.

"I told you to help Mister Jeremiah this morning!" the man barks when Short Bit runs up. He grabs Short Bit's upper arm and hustles him from the barn.

At the same time, Mister Giles strides into the barn, carrying a valise. Walking next to him is a well-dressed gentleman that I recognize as Doctor Crown, Jackson's boss. "Are you dressed and ready, Gabriel?" Mister Giles calls down the aisle.

"Almost, sir." I lead Aristo from the stall for their inspection. The colt's acting high and mighty, and I can tell that Mister Giles is pleased. "Sir, I think I know who timed Aristo the other day. It was Mister Baker!"

Mister Giles gives Doctor Crown a knowing look. Then Mister Giles says in a low voice, "I believe you're right, Gabriel. There have been rumors that Mister Baker was responsible for setting the fire. People are saying that he was paid off by a wealthy, unscrupulous owner who has a horse entered in the Saratoga Chase. We'll make sure The Saratoga Association looks into your information and the accusations."

I nod, glad that the truth will soon be known. "Mister Giles, I have a favor to ask," I say as I lead Aristo past him and Doctor Crown one more time. "'Risto has grown right fond of his groom."

"Short Bit?"

"Yes sir. But Mister Baker just ordered Short Bit to work for another owner."

"I'll talk to Mister Baker right away and let him know that we need Short Bit for the race today."

"And sir…" I press on, knowing I'm taking liberties, but also knowing what I need to ask my boss. "I think it would be a big help if Short Bit came back to Woodville with us. Could you hire the boy from Mister Baker? The farm is always in need of grooms. And you have my word that Short Bit is one of the finest."

He chuckles. "Your sincerity has convinced me. I'll see what I can work out with Mister Baker. In the meantime, get dressed. The bugle will call us to the track at any moment." He hands me the valise.

"Yes sir." I lead Aristo back into his stall, latch it behind me, and hurry to a spare stall. Humming with excitement, I slip on the red silk shirt. Slowly I button it, enjoying the feel of the fabric against my skin. Next I step into the creamy-white britches, lacing them tight around my stomach. Then I slide my feet into my new boots, polished to a shine. Last I set my gold jockey cap on my head, tilting it over my forehead.

I'm ready for this race.

Swinging open the door, I swagger from the stall.

I stop dead in my tracks. Aristo's door is ajar.

"Hey!" I break into a run.

The door flings wide and Hooks flies from the stall, casting me a look I can't understand. I chase him down the aisle, but I ain't no match in my new riding boots. He scoots around the corner of the barn.

I race back to Aristo's stall. The horse is looking at me, bright-eyed. Quickly, I check his feed bucket. It's empty. I throw out the water in his other bucket, and then I poke my fingers inside his mouth, looking for a poisoned apple or opium-laced sugar lump. His mouth is clean.

What then? I rack my brain as I lift his mane and peer under his lip. What did Hooks do to Aristo? Or did I chase him out in time?

Then it hits me: The expression on Hooks's face was one of *smug satisfaction.* Which means he *did* do something to Aristo. Now it all makes sense. Hooks' boss, Cornelius

Jeremiah, has a colt in the Saratoga Chase. *He's* the rich, unscrupulous owner Mister Giles was talking about. He probably paid Mister Baker to set fire to the barn and to hustle Short Bit away from Aristo's stall so that Hooks could sneak in and…and…do what? *What did Hooks do to Aristo?*

My cheeks grow hot. If something happens to the colt, I'll never forgive myself. I should have made sure Angel or Mister Giles was watching him while I dressed.

Rocking on my boot heels, I moan in despair. If only Pa were here!

But Pa ain't here. This is my race. My fight.

Aristo swings his head around, his eyes trusting. I trail my fingers softly down his beautiful face. "What did Hooks do to you?" I ask. Then I grow silent and watchful. Slowly, I circle him, and I listen…and then *I know.*

Aristo's breathing is off. His chest is moving in and out with effort. I press my palm against his ribs, then tilt my head so my ear touches his muzzle. I hear a *hunh* when he breathes out, and a *whrr* when he breathes in. The stall's dim, and when I bend to look closer, Aristo shies into the corner.

"Whoa, horse. Quit being peevish," I scold.

Time's running out. I've got to figure out what's wrong before the race.

A handful of carrots convinces Aristo to stand still while I peer at his muzzle. Something's packed up into his left nostril! Gently, I probe with one finger and pluck out a wad of cotton. Amazed, I stare at it. I knew there were lots of ways to sabotage a racehorse, but this beats anything I ever heard of. These Northern boys have come up with something new this time.

Carefully I pluck out the other wad and step back. Aristo shakes himself like a wet dog and then paws the straw, anxious to get going.

I bow my head in humble thanks, then quickly tack him up.

Mister Giles meets us at the doorway of the barn, Short Bit in tow. "Your groom is at your service," he says.

"Short Bit's coming back to Woodville with us?" I ask.

"I offered him the job." Mister Giles and I both look at Short Bit, who's bobbing his head so rapidly, it appears his neck is on a spring.

"I gather that means yes?" I ask. Grinning, Short Bit takes the reins. "Come on then, Bit. Let's go win a race."

Mister Giles boosts me into the tiny racing saddle. I tell him about Hooks and my suspicions about Mister Jeremiah. His expression turns serious. "Thank you for watching out for Aristo and averting a grave problem, Gabriel. Now we need to get our sights on winning this race. You've got high competition on the track."

"Sir?"

"Gilpatrick's riding Faraway, and Abe's riding Lizzie H."

I suck in my breath. "Then I'm racing against the *best!*"

"Yes." He places his hand on the ankle of my boot. "I have faith in you, Gabriel. I believe you're the right jockey to show these Northerners what a Kentucky-bred boy and a Kentucky-bred colt can do."

"Yes sir." The reply catches in my throat.

I'm silent as Short Bit leads me from the Trotting Course. I'm an inexperienced colored boy, barely free. Why do I think I can win this race against two of the best?

We reach the Saratoga track in time for the judges' inspection and weigh in. Mister Giles leaves to find his seat in the grandstand. As the bell rings, I gather my reins and Short Bit unhooks the lead. When he steps away, I steer Aristo toward the gap in the railing.

"Gabriel?" Short Bit calls. I twist in the saddle, trying to spot the boy in the throng of grown-ups. But then he waves hesitantly, and calls, "Good luck!" For the first time since we met, I see hope in his eyes. I touch the brim of my cap in a salute.

Then Aristo breaks into a jig, and I lose sight of Short Bit as we follow Abe Hawkins and Lizzie H. through the gap and onto the track. As we jog by the grandstand, I stare slack-jawed at the crowd. The grandstand is full of ladies waving handkerchiefs. The lawn is packed with men in suits, and the railings on both sides are bursting with men and boys in work clothes.

Unsettled by the uproar, Aristo dances nervously. My own nerves are stretched tight; my wits feel addled. The Kentucky Association meets were nothing like this grand affair!

Cornelius Jeremiah's colt Faraway trots past, his chestnut coat gleaming, and his jockey Gilpatrick basks in the hoorahs from the grandstand. Then Abe canters past on Lizzie H. He waves his whip at the onlookers, who chant his name. Then the stewards ring the bell again, summoning us to the starting line.

I steer Aristo around. "Go back to Kentucky!" a man yells at me from the grandstand. I seek out his face, finding hundreds that seem to glare at me.

My stomach rolls and I inhale raggedly. Then I spy Jackson with Miss Lacey from Moon's Lake House. He's hanging over the railing, waving two betting tickets in the air.

"Win for us, Gabriel!" he yells across the noise.

Aristo tosses his head. I place my palm on his warm neck. I feel his muscles ripple beneath my fingers.

Can we win?

Moments later, the horses line up between the judges' towers. On my left are Faraway, Lizzie H., and a colt named Townsend. On my right is a white-eyed mare named Susannah.

The steward dashes in front of us, watching to see when the horses' front legs are even. I twine two fingers in Aristo's mane. The colt's front hooves dance. He's bound to break fast.

"Go!" The judges holler, the drum taps, and Aristo rears as the other four horses break from the starting line.

I fall back, my hold on Aristo's mane the only thing keeping me from plummeting to the ground. The colt springs forward, throwing me onto his neck, then charges after the others.

The crowd jeers as we pass.

Gasping, I find my stirrups and my balance. The colt's running wild around the backstretch turn, bent on catching up even if his heart bursts. Hastily, I take up the slack in the rein and steady him between my hands.

"Easy, 'Risto," I croon, but the wind tosses my words to the sky.

Five lengths ahead, I see four tails streaming in a ragged line. I grit my teeth. Aristo's the greatest horse, but it will be impossible to catch up!

Then I hear Jackson's words: *Don't ever give up on those dreams.*

Determination fills me. I want to *win* this race. I want to show Mister Baker and Mister Jeremiah that all their cheating can't stop us. I want to show these jeering Northerners what a Kentucky boy and colt can do. I want my name written in a newspaper for all to read. And I want to win because racing and winning's in my blood, and because *this is what I was born to do.*

Jackson's right. I *am* like him. Galloping Aristo, the wind slapping my face, is as close to heaven as a boy can get. *This* is my freedom. And winning *is* possible!

I chirp, and the colt surges forward like water rushing in a swollen river. Ahead of us, Townsend is falling behind. Aristo passes him on the outside like the other horse is walking.

Now we're three lengths behind.

The crowd whoops gaily as the horses thunder down the homestretch to finish the first lap. We're close enough now that I can see Lizzie H. and Faraway battling for the lead. Susannah's running flat, so it won't be long before we catch her.

We round the homestretch turn, passing Susannah and gaining on Lizzie H. Abe glances over his shoulder and his eyes meet mine. He raises that whip. *Whap, whap, whap,* he pummels Lizzie's flank.

"Take her, 'Risto," I whisper into the colt's flying mane.

As we pull past Lizzie, Abe flashes me a crooked grin like he knows Aristo's meant to win. Like he knows it's *my* turn. Now Faraway's the only horse between us and the finish line.

And I'm bound and determined to beat that no-account Cornelius Jeremiah.

I edge my hands higher, slackening the rein, and nudge my heels against Aristo's sides. The colt hurtles down the track. He runs like he's playing in the field at Woodville Farm. Runs like the rebel raiders are after him. Runs because it's in his heart, and this is what *he* was born to do. I glance left at Faraway, who's flagging. Gilpatrick spurs him, but Faraway's sides are heaving.

I close my eyes. *Huff, huff, huff!* The colt's telling me he ain't quite winded. He forges ahead and joy rises in my chest.

Hooks and Cuffy's meanness. Danny and Gordon's threats. Mister Baker's fire. Mister Jeremiah's sabotage. The odds were against us, but it made no difference.

Aristo's unstoppable. *Unbeatable.*

We fly across the finish line. I pump my fist in the air, and the crowd chants my name: *"Gabriel! Gabriel! Gabriel!"*

A smile cracks my dusty cheeks. "We won, 'Risto." I stroke my hand down the colt's sweaty neck. He slows to a trot and I rein him around. Reporters are streaming onto the track, pads in their hands, and their eyes are on *me*.

I only wish Pa and Ma were here to see.

At that moment, Abe jogs past on Lizzie H. He's tired and defeated, but there's a shadow of a smile on his face. He nods at me one time before disappearing into the oncoming throng.

"Gabriel Alexander!" the first reporter to reach me hollers. "You triumphed over Abe Hawkins and Gilpatrick, two of the greatest riders in the world. How'd you do it?"

"*I* didn't do it," I reply breathlessly. "It was my horse, sir. *Aristo.* He's the greatest. He told me how to ride him. All I had to do was listen."

Suddenly reporters and stewards surround us, all calling out at once, writing down my name on their pads. Then I spot Mister Giles, Jackson, and Short Bit pushing through them. They're grinning to beat the band, and I sit tall in the saddle.

I won this race for Mister Giles. I won it to show the world that Aristo's the finest horse. I won it so Jackson, Ma, and Pa would be proud of me. I won it so Annabelle would read my name in the paper.

I raise my arm and wave to the grandstand. The crowd is on its feet and roaring. Aristo tosses his head, skitters sideways, and the reporters scatter. I grin so big my cheeks hurt.

I know I won this race for me, too. Fame and winning feel so powerful they're bursting my head wide. But now I realize that this triumph is not the end of my journey.

It is only the beginning.

THE HISTORY BEHIND GABRIEL'S TRIUMPH

Kentucky African Americans
and the Union Army

In 1863, Abraham Lincoln issued the Emancipation Proclamation, freeing many of the slaves in the United States. But in several border states like Kentucky, Lincoln allowed citizens loyal to the Union to continue to own slaves.

From the beginning of the Civil War, the Union army could impress (force into service) both free and slave black men for labor. While the impressed black men did not serve in battle, they performed tasks such as driving wagons or building military roads. Many impressed Negro men helped build Camp Nelson, Kentucky. As

Union army wagon drivers

the Civil War raged on, white recruits grew scarce. The Union army desperately needed more soldiers, so they decided to allow black men—free or slave—to enlist. In July 1864, when Gabriel's father joined the army, many black men in Kentucky left their homes and families to become soldiers. At Camp Nelson, about 5,405 slaves were recruited into the Union army.

White slave owners in Kentucky reacted strongly, sometimes violently, to losing their workers. "Soon after the introduction of colored recruits into the camps," wrote Thomas Butler of the U.S. Sanitary Commission, "their old owners came in carriages and on horseback every day to allure them by all kinds of promises and threats, and in many cases to kidnap them back into bondage." Joseph

Holt, head of the Bureau of Military Justice, wrote: "Slaves escaping from their masters with a view of entering military service were waylaid, beaten, maimed and often murdered."

Black families at Camp Nelson

Many of the wives and children of the new black recruits suffered, too. Some of them ran away from their owners and followed their husbands to Camp Nelson. Others were thrown off their farms by angry owners. At first, some of the Union army commanders tried to feed and shelter the refugees:

"General Thomas' instructions are to discourage as far as possible negro women and children coming into camp. Such as come however must be provided for." (June 30, 1864).

Camp Nelson employed some of the women, like Gabriel's mother, to cook and wash. But living conditions for the refugees were miserable. The families lived in tents and shanties, and had little food and supplies. As refugees continued to pour into Camp Nelson, the commanders changed their orders: "All negro women and children, except those who have written permits from these Head Qurs...will be expelled from Camp on Monday Sept.19 '64."

Saratoga Springs, New York

When Gabriel traveled north to Saratoga Springs, New York, he wasn't aware of the town's history. The Native Americans called the area *Sarachtogue* (or *Sa-ragh-to-ga)*, which means "place of the swift river." They hunted game in the forests and used the mineral springs as medicine. After the Revolutionary War white families settled nearby, and the healing springs attracted many tourists to the area.

Saratoga Springs's first hotel was built in 1802. The town drew famous figures of the time, such as Daniel Webster and Andrew Jackson. People traveled up the Hudson River on steamers or on trains, escaping the cities for the summer. They drank from the mineral springs, hoping to cure their ailments. The springs were manned by dipper boys. The boys placed cups in baskets on the end of long poles and dipped them into the springs. "Its use is prescribed by physicians," boasted a travel brochure. Although many visitors praised the water for its healing qualities, some people spat out the water because of the unpleasant taste!

During the 1860s, Saratoga Springs was a popular destination for people weary of the hardships of wartime. Some called the lively town the "greatest escape." Shops sold fancy goods, and theaters featured sideshows and operas.

There were bowling alleys and a ride called the Circular Railway. Grand hotels—several of them five stories tall and large enough to sleep 2,000 guests— lined the main street.

Grand Union Hotel, Saratoga

The resort attracted millionaires and powerful politicians, including state governors. "Bob" Lincoln, Abraham Lincoln's son, stayed at Union Hall, where he danced to the music of a twenty-two piece band. On August 5, "the biggest party in the country" was held in the Union Hall's dining room. As reported by the *New York Herald,* the guests were served a "supper worthy of the gods."

Horse Racing in Saratoga Springs

Saratoga Springs is the home of the Saratoga Race Course. It is America's oldest major sports facility. In 1863, in the middle of the Civil War, the new racetrack's first meet attracted a crowd of around 5,000. It was such a success that plans were made to build a new track. In July 1864, when Gabriel and Aristo arrived in Saratoga Springs, the new racetrack was ready. It had a covered grandstand to seat well-to-do ladies in hoop skirts and men in stove-pipe hats. "General admission" spectators watched the races from the open-air bleachers. Ordinary tickets cost fifty cents; grandstand tickets were one dollar. Although African Americans rode, trained, and groomed the racehorses, they were not allowed in the seating areas.

The Saratoga Chase, Gabriel's race on Aristo, is fictional. But the meet at Saratoga Springs, which ran from August 2 to August 6 in 1864, was real. The famous white jockey Gilbert W. Patrick (popularly known as Gilpatrick) and the equally famous ex-slave jockey Abe Hawkins battled in the Travers race and the Sequel Stakes. The meet's last race was the Congress Spring Purse. It was a marathon race of three 3-mile heats.

Grandstand, Saratoga Race Course

The horses ran full speed for a total of nineteen minutes with thirty minutes to rest between each heat.

On July 30 of that year, while Saratoga Springs was preparing for the races, the bloody Battle of the Crater was raging in Petersburg, Virginia. The attack turned out to be a failure for the North. The Union lost 3,393 soldiers. The Confederates lost 1,500. After the battle, Abraham Lincoln declared the first Thursday of August (August 4, 1864) as a Day of Prayer. In his proclamation he stated the hope that "unity and fraternity may be restored and peace established throughout all our borders." On that date in Saratoga Springs, however, the war seemed far away. Crowds overflowed the grandstand of the Saratoga Race Course, and, instead of praying, the ladies and gentlemen in attendance cheered for their favorite horses.

Fire!

In the 1800s, most homes, hotels, and shops were built of wood. They were also heated with wood stoves. Barns were made of wood and filled with hay and straw. Fires were common and often deadly. The Great Chicago Fire of 1871 killed 300 people and burned some 17,450 buildings.

In July of 1864, shortly before Gabriel's fictional visit to Saratoga Springs, fireworks set off a blaze on the rear porch

Horse-drawn pumper wagon decorated for a parade

of a store. Buildings along two hundred feet of Broadway burned, including a blacksmith shop, a soap factory, and an ice house. Later, fires destroyed two Saratoga Springs landmarks—the United States Hotel in 1865, and Congress Hall in 1866.

Early fires such as the one at the racetrack stables in the story were often doused by bucket brigades—lines of men and women passing buckets of water from hand to hand. By the time of the Civil War, some larger cities in the United States had fire hydrants and steam pumpers to control fires. Some towns depended on hand pumpers. Firefighters pulled the fire engine near the burning building, then filled a tub with water. They rapidly pushed two handles up and down to pump water from the tub through the heavy hose. A bucket brigade had to work constantly to keep the tub full. The water could only squirt a short distance, so fire engines needed to be very close to the flames.

Note: The quote from Joseph Holt and Thomas Butler as well as the orders concerning refugees from June 1864 and September 1864 came from Richard Sears's book, *Camp Nelson, Kentucky.* The quote from the travel brochure is taken from *Saratoga Lost.* The quote from Abraham Lincoln appeared in his Day of Prayer proclamation *(Proclamation for a Day of Prayer. July 7, 1864. By the President of the United States of America).*

BIBLIOGRAPHICAL NOTE

To research and write the Racing to Freedom Trilogy, I read over two hundred books. The following sources were especially important for Gabriel's Triumph:

BOOKS

Calderone, John A. *History of Fire Engines*. FAJ Publications: 1997.

DelVecchio, Mike. *Railroads Across America*. MBI Publishing Company: 1998

Harter, Jim. *American RR of the Nineteenth Century*. Texas Tech University Press: 1998.

Hollingsworth, Kent. *The Kentucky Thoroughbred*. The University Press of Kentucky: 1976.

Hotaling, Edward. *Great Black Jockeys*. Forum; Rockling, CA: 1999.

Hotaling, Edward. *They're Off! Horse Racing at Saratoga*. Syracuse University Press: 1995.

Joki, Robert. *Saratoga Lost: Images of Victorian America*. Black Dome Press: 1998

Lucas, Marion B. *A History of Kentucky: From Slavery to Segregation, 1760–1891*. Kentucky Historical Society: 2003.

Lucas, Scott J. "High Expectations: African Americans in Civil War Kentucky." *Negro History Bulletin:* Jan/Dec: 2001.

Renau, Lynn S. *Racing Around Kentucky.* Antiques Consultant Inc. Louisville, KY: 1995.

Sears, Richard D. *Camp Nelson, Kentucky.* The University Press of Kentucky: 2002.

WEBSITES

www.saratoga.org
www.campnelson.org
www.kyhistory.org

ABOUT THE AUTHOR

ALISON HART enjoys writing about history and horses, two of her favorite subjects. "I'd love to go back in time," she says, "and meet people like Gabriel who followed their dreams, no matter what the hardships." Researching GABRIEL'S TRIUMPH took her to the Bluegrass region of Kentucky and its rich Thoroughbred racing and Civil War history. She soon realized that the suspenseful story of Gabriel and his family wouldn't fit in one book. The other titles in the Racing to Freedom trilogy are GABRIEL'S HORSES and the upcoming GABRIEL'S JOURNEY.

Ms. Hart, a teacher and author, has written more than twenty books for children and young adults. Many of her titles—including ANNA'S BLIZZARD, an IRA Teacher's Choice and WILLA Finalist, and SHADOW HORSE, an Edgar Nominee—feature horses. Her historical mystery FIRES OF JUBILEE is also set at the time of the Civil War.